CONTENTS

Title Page
Copyright
Dedication

CHAPTER ONE	1
CHAPTER TWO	8
CHAPTER THREE	13
CHAPTER FOUR	19
CHAPTER FIVE	31
CHAPTER SIX	35
CHAPTER SEVEN	38
CHAPTER EIGHT	40
CHAPTER NINE	42
CHAPTER TEN	46
CHAPTER ELEVEN	49
CHAPTER TWELVE	52
CHAPTER THIRTEEN	54
CHAPTER FOURTEEN	56

CHAPTER FIFTEEN	57
CHAPTER SIXTEEN	62
CHAPTER SEVENTEEN	68
CHAPTER EIGHTEEN	70
CHAPTER NINETEEN	76
CHAPTER TWENTY	92
CHAPTER TWENTY-ONE	94
CHAPTER TWENTY-TWO	96
CHAPTER TWENTY-THREE	104
CHAPTER TWENTY-FOUR	108
CHAPTER TWENTY-FIVE	113
CHAPTER TWENTY-SIX	116
CHAPTER TWENTY-SEVEN	118
CHAPTER TWENTY-EIGHT	120
CHAPTER TWENTY-NINE	122
CHAPTER THIRTY	127
CHAPTER THIRTY-ONE	129
CHAPTER THIRTY-TWO	133
CHAPTER THIRTY-THREE	136
CHAPTER THIRTY-FOUR	140
CHAPTER THIRTY-FIVE	142
CHAPTER THIRTY-SIX	146
CHAPTER THIRTY-SEVEN	150
CHAPTER THIRTY-EIGHT	155

CHAPTER THIRTY-NINE	159
CHAPTER FORTY	162
CHAPTER FORTY-ONE	165
CHAPTER FORTY-TWO	168
CHAPTER FORTY-THREE	170
CHAPTER FORTY-FOUR	172
CHAPTER FORTY-FIVE	173
CHAPTER FORTY-SIX	179
CHAPTER FORTY-SEVEN	181
CHAPTER FORTY-EIGHT	185
CHAPTER FORTY-NINE	190
CHAPTER FIFTY	192
CHAPTER FIFTY-ONE	196
CHAPTER FIFTY-TWO	199
CHAPTER FIFTY-THREE	205
CHAPTER FIFTY-FOUR	212
CHAPTER FIFTY-FIVE	214
CHAPTER FIFTY-SIX	225
CHAPTER FIFTY-SEVEN	229
CHAPTER FIFTY-EIGHT	231
CHAPTER FIFTY-NINE	237
Afterword	243
Want More?	245
Book 2: Can't Let My Heart Fall	247

Books In This Series	257
Books By This Author	263

THE LOVE OF A LORD

Rebecca Paulinyi

Copyright © 2021 Rebecca Paulinyi

All rights reserved

This is a work of fiction. Names, characters, businesses, places, events and incidents are either the products of the author's imagination or used in a fictitious manner. Any resemblance to actual persons, living or dead, or actual events is purely coincidental.

No part of this book may be reproduced, or stored in a retrieval system, or transmitted in any form or by any means, electronic, mechanical, photocopying, recording, or otherwise, without express written permission of the publisher.

Cover design by: GM Book Covers Design

*For my mum: thank you for everything
you do, every single day.*

To hear about new releases, see pictures of my dog and generally hear about my writing, you can sign up to my newsletter here: tiny.cc/paulinyi

CHAPTER ONE
Annelise

Mist rose steadily from the lake like a ghost, seeping into the air, the trees, the flowers. I couldn't pull myself away, despite the way the chill seeped into my very bones, my dress clinging damply to my shivering form.

This witch's cauldron of a lake stood in the shadow of the magnificent manor house, the manor house my mother had started her working life in. It was also the place she had been travelling to when she had met with that fateful accident.

I didn't know what had brought me here except some morbid desire to feel somewhat closer to my mother - and I didn't know what would drag me away.

"You'll freeze to death!" A voice permeated the mists around me and I blinked once, twice, coming out of my trance and seeing for the first time the outline of a man coming towards me. He wore a black cloak, although I doubted it did much to stop the driving rain that had begun, and was taking long, purposeful strides towards me.

"Can you not feel this storm?" he asked; somehow his strong voice was not whisked away on the racing wind. "Come away from there!"

I nodded mutely, seeming to only then realise how truly cold I was in my thin dress and leaking boots, and took a step towards him, the manor looming as his backdrop.

My feet, soaked through and still for so long, however, seemed to have forgotten how to work properly, and as my body moved forwards and my legs did not, I felt my whole body fall.

Only for a second though; strong, warm hands caught my shoulder and heaved me back upright. Before I could make sense of what was happening, he'd sighed loudly - he was so close I could hear it over the roar of the wind - and put one arm beneath my knees, sweeping me off my feet and into his arms.

It all happened so quickly; I didn't get a chance to think about how indecent it was. Instead, I marvelled at how the warmth of his body reached me through the layers of soaking clothes between us, and how his long strides made quick work of the distance across the grounds to the main house.

Straight through the front door he carried

me; I was sure I'd never been through anything other than the servants' door in such a grand house.

I barely had time to admire the intricate paintings on the walls or the gleaming wooden floors; he kicked open a door off from the main hall and walked into a cosy sitting room. A fire was lit in the great stone fireplace and I could feel the heat even from the other side of the room.

I realised I had not yet asked him what he was doing - but I could not seem to make my tongue work properly. Perhaps my brain was addled from the cold.

More gently than I'd expected, he lowered me onto a footstool in front of the fire. The wind battered and buffeted the house, making the glass visibly shake in its panes, but the warmth of the fire felt as though it thawed me - my legs, my mind and finally my tongue.

He found his first.

"What on Earth were you doing? Do you want to catch a chill? Or lose a leg?"

I was aware I was dripping on his very expensive-looking floors, but I couldn't see that there was anything I could do about it. "I was distracted," I said, finally finding my voice.

He looked incredulous. "Distracted! What a

reason to endanger your life." He reached for a bell. "You'll need to change out of those clothes if we're to mitigate the damage."

A young girl appeared almost instantly, and I listened as he made his wishes clear. "She'll need a clean set of clothes," he said, jerking his head towards me. "Go through Mary's belongings, if you need to. And some wine, please."

"Yes, sir," she said, leaving the room as silently as she'd entered it, and I couldn't help but imagine my mother here. She would have been the serving girl in this scenario - not sat like I was, in front of the fire, having clothes brought to me.

The world was indeed a very strange place.

"Can you tell me your name?" he asked, a little more softly this time, as if I were some terrified creature who might faint in fright.

I supposed I did look a little woeful.

"Annelise," I said, noticing my teeth had stopped chattering. "Annelise Edwards."

"And what were you doing out in the pouring rain, Annelise?" I found I liked the way my name sounded as it fell from his lips. His voice was so sure, so strong, so confident - like nothing I had ever heard before. His dark black hair fell in waves around his shoulders, and although he had been in the rain like I had, it was nowhere near as sodden as every inch of me.

"I took a trip to see the gardens," I said. "I'd heard they were wonderful." It wasn't too far from the truth, although I didn't mention the fact that my mother had been a servant here, worried I would instantly destroy this strange dynamic between us.

"In a storm?" he asked, his brow furrowed as if he could not quite work me out.

"There wasn't a storm when I left," I said. Then, I felt a little more daring, as though the warmth of the fire were giving me some of my strength back. "And what is your name?"

He smirked, just for a moment. "Nicholas," he said. That was all; Nicholas. No surname, no title, although if this were his house I was sure he would have one. From the little my mother had told me of her time here, I knew he had not been in charge back then; but then surely he could only be approaching thirty, too young to have been in charge of a grand house the twenty years or so ago when my mother had worked here. Perhaps the master was his father - but I did not know how to ask that without revealing more of myself than I wished.

The serving girl reappeared with two glasses of wine, and a neat pile of clothing. He absented himself from the room with little fuss, and I smiled as the girl offered to help me. I did not know if it were the weather or the warmth from the fire, but my head was beginning to spin.

Once I had divested myself of my thin, wet dress, I realised my undergarments were also too wet to continue wearing. A blush came to my cheeks as I stripped off, but the girl did not comment or even really look. The shift she handed me was of a finer quality than I had ever worn, and although I felt like an impostor, what choice did I have? Nicholas was right - I would be ill if I stayed in those wet clothes.

Then a dress, fairly simple but clearly of expensive fabric, in a beautiful cloth that reminded me of the sky on a cloudless day. I wondered who Mary was, that these clothes belonged to - his wife, perhaps? Or sister? I hated that I hoped it were the latter. What a ridiculous thought that it might matter, either way.

And then she was gone, and I was once more sat in front of the fire, letting my eyes drift closed as a haze of tiredness, cold and frustration washed over me. Why had mother been so desperate to come here, when she was ailing herself? Why had she pushed herself so hard she had fallen to her death from some borrowed horse, mere miles away? My grief had not subsided in the months since her passing, and the anger at her actions was an unwelcome addition to the mix.

"Drink some wine." The sudden sound of his voice brought me back to the moment, and I opened my eyes and took a glass, with what I hoped was a grateful smile.

It was warm, and spiced, and the feeling of it burning down my throat and accosting my nose finally started to remove the chill that I was worried had become permanent. He sipped from his goblet, his eyes on mine, but I felt too tired to do anything but sit and drink and let my eyes be lost in his.

I had never been alone with a man before; and certainly never in the same room as someone so devastatingly handsome as Nicholas. It wasn't just the dark hair; it was the way his clothes fitted his muscled form, the way his eyes flashed when he was angry or frustrated, the way his full lips pressed together to stop some thought from passing them.

I knew I was unlikely to ever see this man - or one who would rival his looks - again in my little lifetime, and so I let the fact that I was exhausted and my hair was still soaking go from my mind, and drank in the image of him, as he tried to understand this strange woman who was sat in his sitting room.

CHAPTER TWO
Nicholas

Her gaze was a little too intense to be comfortable, and I moved my gaze to the fire when I could no longer stand it. She was a mystery, this mousy-haired girl who I had feared would be swept into the lake during this terrible storm. Now, sat in one of my sister's old day dresses that she had left here when she had married, she looked more presentable - but still I did not feel I understood her motives.

I took another sip of the hot, spiced wine that had been brought, and felt it warm me to my bones. I had not been out in the storm for long; far less time than she had. Thankfully I had seen her as I looked out of the window, and managed to bring her inside. The last thing I needed was a dead body surfacing in the lake. There was already enough gossip about me, about how long Marvale had stood empty even though I had inherited it, and my title, when my father died three years previously. Gossip about the fact that I had been due to marry at the beginning of the year, only to be jilted for another, much wealthier man.

Yes, there was enough for the locals to whisper about me, without a body surfacing on my property.

"Are you feeling warmer?" I asked, and she nodded, her face blushing prettily. There were curls in her mousy hair, but I did not know if they were thanks to the soaking from outside. She spoke with a slight accent, perhaps from London - but that was as much as I could figure out. I was used to reading people much more easily than this, and it frustrated me.

"Are you staying locally?" I asked, wanting to at least find out if my hunch about her home was correct.

"I-" She faltered, and I wondered why such a question would throw her off. "I have not yet secured lodgings," she said finally, smoothing an imaginary crease in the borrowed dress and avoiding my eye line.

"So you came to tour the gardens, and did not have somewhere to stay?"

"Indeed." She did not look at me, but her cheeks flushed further. Something wasn't quite truthful about her words, I was sure - but then from recent experience, I was inclined to doubt any and all women.

"Well," I said, feeling like I would quite like to solve this mystery. "You cannot go back out in this weather." She turned to face the window, her face falling, as she saw that the weather was just as bad - or possibly worse - than when we had entered the house.

She turned back, slowly shaking her head. "I suppose not."

"Stay for dinner," I said, not sure where the words or the desire to offer had come from. "And then I will direct you to the nearest inn, once the weather is less vicious."

Her eyebrows raised a little, but she nodded her head. I would get to the bottom of why she had come, I decided as I drained my glass, and then I could send her on her way. I would have forgotten about her as soon as she was out of sight - but for now, a distraction from my own company might not be such a bad thing. After all, I had dined alone so many nights I had lost count.

"Well, I must change," I said, standing and turning on my heel to the door. "Make yourself comfortable."

The warmth of the fire was sadly lacking when I left the small room, and as I climbed the stairs I could not help but notice all the things that had fallen into disrepair. I needed to find the time - and the inclination - to restore Marvale to the glory it deserved. Since Father had died, I had not dedicated any time at all to my childhood home - and then, when I had planned to marry, I had foolishly thought to leave things until my wife could have a say in how her home would look.

And now I was not married, and the place still needed work, and the issue was not a lack of coin. No, the family coffers were plentiful, and I was embarrassed at myself for letting Marvale become run down when I was perfectly capable of making the place beautiful.

Thank goodness my sister Mary had not visited in the last couple of years; I think it might have broken her heart.

"Good evening, sir." I startled a little as I entered my bedchamber, not expecting Harris to be there. He had been working here since I was a little boy, but when I had offered him retirement he had declined. I had no idea how old he was - I wasn't even sure he knew - but he seemed happy working here, and I wasn't going to take that away from him. Besides, it was rather comforting to have someone working here who had known me before I was the master of the house.

"Evening, Harris," I said. "I just need to change, got caught in the storm." Before I even had chance to finish my sentence, he was laying out a dry pair of hose and a fresh shirt, and I smiled in thanks.

As he turned to leave, I had a sudden thought. "Oh, there's a young lady in the sitting room. Can you get one of the maids to help her with her hair? She was caught in the storm too."

He nodded, unquestioning as always, and I stripped off, wishing I had thought to have the fire lit in here. The wind found its way through every crack it could find, and it was anything but cosy as I hurried to redress myself. A hearty dinner, and some wine by the fireplace would surely warm me up - and once I had figured out the mystery behind Annelise's tale, she would be on her way and I could get back to the work I should have been doing today.

CHAPTER THREE
Annelise

I had jumped and squeaked something nonsensical when a fairly young maid - younger than me, anyway - had appeared and said something about sorting my hair. Other than my mother, no-one had ever fixed my hair but me - but she seemed to be under orders, and I didn't want to get her in trouble with anyone. Despite the heat of the fire, it was still damp from the terrible rain, which seemed to be showing no signs of abating.

"I'm Annelise," I told her as she turned me so my hair was closer to the fire and pulled the brush carefully through my hair. As always happened when it got wet, curls had sprung up throughout it, and leaving it loose on such a vile day had clearly been a terrible idea.

"I'm Edith, m'lady," she said. I could not help but wince as she pulled the brush, no matter how gentle she was trying to be, and she apologised.

"It's fine," I said, wanting to correct her assumption that I was someone with a title, someone who belonged in this world - but realising if I did, Nicholas was bound to hear of it. If I could make it through dinner without him throwing me out due my poor background, perhaps I could find some information, some lead, to help me discover why on earth my mother had been so insistent on travelling here, as frail as she was.

Despite feeling guilty for pretending to be more important than I was, I began to relax into the repetitive motion of the brush through my hair, especially once she had worked through the knots. The fire and the movement seemed to be drying it, and I realised my eyes had fluttered closed as her hands worked through my thick hair. I was exhausted, from the travel, from the cold, and now from a lack of a decent meal.

"That acceptable, m'lady?" she asked, and I reached up to find my hair in an intricate plait.

"Wonderful," I said. "Thank you."

"Dinner will be served any minute," she said. "I'll show you the way."

It was the finest dining hall I'd ever seen, but then that wasn't saying much. Dark, thick, wooden beams criss-crossed above us and a huge table - far too large for two people - sat in the middle. Candles were lit all the way down the table, and although it was not that late the storm had added a gloominess that was hard to see in. A fire roared in the grate, and Nicholas sat in a chair at the head of the table, looking every bit as breathtakingly handsome as he had in the small room by the fire.

I had hoped my imagination had been exaggerating.

He stood as I entered, pulling out the chair beside him, and I was relieved it was just to be the two of us. Fewer people meant fewer lies - although I could not help but wonder if he had a wife, or children. Not that it would change anything - but I did feel a burning desire to know.

I smiled shyly, and he smiled back, just for a moment, before a steaming dish of soup was brought in. After hours without food it smelt heavenly, and when he gestured for me to start I did not hesitate. Warm, freshly baked bread was brought in next, and it was the most delicious thing I had ever tasted.

For a few moments we ate in silence, and I tried to remember my table manners in spite of my hunger, reminding myself that I was dining with someone who was most probably a lord - even if he had not told me his title.

When the silence stretched on a little longer than was comfortable, I decided to be brave and ask a question.

"Have you lived here long?"

He waited until he had finished his mouthful, and took a long sip of the wine that had been brought to us. "A few months," he said. "Although I grew up here."

"Where have you been in between?" I asked, knowing it was rude but finding this man who had pulled me in from a storm intriguing.

"Here and there," he said, waving his hand in the air. "Most recently, court."

My eyes widened. "Did you meet the King?"

He laughed; "I did, in fact. And the Queen."

Definitely a lord, then, at least - and I felt awed by the idea that he had been in the presence of the most powerful man in the country.

I had nothing I could respond to that, and so instead took several sips of the wine. It was not warm, nor spiced, but tasted equally delicious. And as an impressive stuffed bird was brought out and carved before us, I was sure this was to be the richest, most decadent meal of my life.

"So," he said, tapping his fingers gently on the wooden table. "What else did you have planned for today, other than touring the gardens?"

I took a mouthful of food at that moment,

a good excuse to think through my answer. If I wanted him to help me, I would need to give him something... but I was also not convinced that, if he found out I was the daughter of a servant, he would be particularly inclined to help me. Not if he fraternised with royalty...

"I was supposed to be tracing a friend of mine," I said. "She went missing in this area."

"I'm sorry to hear that," he said, and I wasn't sure he was entirely convinced. "Perhaps I've heard of her?"

I shook my head. "I doubt it. But then I heard about the garden, and the rain..." I felt overly hot, all of a sudden, and took a gulp of wine - although I wasn't sure it was helping. The borrowed dress felt tight and the food sat heavy in my stomach. He was speaking, but I couldn't make my mind focus on the words coming from his lips.

Air. I needed air, I needed something to get me back in control of my senses. Surely rich food could not make me ill so quickly? Or perhaps he was right about getting caught in that terrible storm...

"Excuse me," I said, jumping up from the table, probably interrupting him mid-sentence, but knowing I needed to get away from the food and the fire.

I stumbled into the hallway, the cold air hitting me like a battering ram, but it did not help. The buzzing in my head grew stronger, and as I reached out for the bannister to help me stand, everything faded to black.

CHAPTER FOUR
Nicholas

I waited for a few moments, confused as to what had just happened. Was she just trying to escape my interrogation? It seemed pretty clear she was lying, but I did not think I had been particularly forceful, and there was certainly no need for her to run from the room.

When she did not reappear with a smile or a word of apology, I pushed my chair backwards and strode into the hallway - and then I gasped, seeing her lying in a heap on the floor.

I ran, then, and thanked God that she did not seem to have hit her head on the flagstones.

"Harris!" I shouted, and the old man appeared in an instant, his face in shock at the scene.

"She's fainted," I said, stating the obvious. "I'm taking her to the Blue Room. Send one of the girls to tend to her, please." And with that I swept her off the floor and into my arms - for the second time that day.

Her weight was nothing, but I was concerned with how hot she felt to the touch. Had I been too late, pulling her in from the storm, and she now had a fever? It seemed the only conclusion - unless she had been ill when she arrived, but she hadn't seemed it. Well, except for her ridiculous behaviour of staring into a lake in the middle of a storm.

I kicked the door open, and managed to balance her with an arm and a knee so I could pull back the bed linens and lay her down. She would need to be undressed, and probably bathed with cool water, but that was certainly no job for me.

No, she would not want me here while she was in this state, and I certainly did not want to be taking care of some woman. Women always brought trouble - and this one seemed to be no exception.

◆ ◆ ◆

My appetite had gone, and the food was cold, but I did not wish to waste the meal that had been prepared for us. I finished as much as I could, along with more wine than was strictly sensible, and pondered the strange turn my day had taken. Somehow I had gone from a perfectly normal day to having a mysterious woman in the bedroom opposite mine. And the last thing I wanted was a woman to be my responsibility again.

No, hopefully she could sleep off whatever illness she had caught and be well enough to send to an inn - or to where she hailed from - in the morning. Never mind the mystery behind why she was here, or the obvious lie about a missing friend - I needed to know I had only myself to look after.

I wasn't even particularly sure I was capable of doing that.

I took myself to bed early, taking another glass of wine and a book to read by the candlelight. I wasn't especially tired - the storm had stopped me riding into the village to see what the housing was like, as I had planned to - but I just wanted to hide away from the storm and stay warm.

It was about an hour after I'd settled under the covers when I heard it. A scream, for certain, followed by a yelp. I jumped out of bed, grabbing the candle to light the dark corridor, and for a moment stood in the doorway, heart thundering in my ears, trying to figure out where it had come from.

"No! No! No!" The Blue Room, of course; opposite my chamber and the location of Annelise. I paused to knock at the door, but the scream from inside made me dispatch with politeness and simply barge in. It sounded like she was being attacked, and I could not afford to waste a moment.

I burst through the door to find her alone, but the look of distress on her face made me shiver. She wore a thin nightdress - one of my sister's, I presumed - that clung to her figure in the shadows of the candlelight. And then she screamed again, but she was not even looking at me; she stared at the ceiling, and I looked up too, but there was nothing there.

"Let me out!" she screamed, and I gathered my senses and rushed to her, placing the candle down on the nightstand.

"Annelise," I said, taking hold of her shoulders to see if I could wake her from whatever nightmare she was having - but her skin was burning to the touch, and she did not seem to be asleep.

She shivered, and I felt panic rising within me. What was the right course of action, when someone had a fever like this? Father had died of a fever, but I had not been there - I did not know...

"It's all right," I said, steering her towards the bed.

"The flames!" she shouted, fanning her hands, looking around wildly. "They're everywhere! We must leave!"

I shushed gently, trying to calm her, although I doubted my words would reach her.

"There's no fire. It's all right."

"I'm so hot..." she moaned, pulling at the neckline of the nightdress, and I averted my eyes, not wanting to see her in a state of undress.

Next to the bed was a bowl of cool water and a linen cloth, and once I'd persuaded her to sit down I soaked it thoroughly, then wrung it out and began to wipe her brow, her cheeks, her neck, hoping the cold water would take away some of the bite of the fever. I ran to open the windows, letting in the cold night air that seemed to have rained itself out, but then dashed back to put a blanket over her so she would not become more ill. Why did I not know what to do? I felt so useless, but she sighed at the feeling of the wash cloth, and so I continued my ministrations.

It was not long before Edith arrived, presumably awoken by the woman's screaming, and if she were surprised to see me here she didn't say anything.

"My lord?"

"Her fever," I said. "It's worse. I think - she's seeing things."

Edith crossed herself, which did not make me feel any better.

"What should I do?" I asked, and she looked a little horrified at being asked.

"Cool water, I think, but don't let the room get too cold." She hurried to close the windows. "Shall I send for a doctor?"

Annelise had leant back against the pillows and closed her eyes, and as much as I was pleased to see she was no longer terrified, her skin was clearly red hot.

"Yes. I think so."

◆ ◆ ◆

I did not know how much time had passed, but I sat there with the cool cloth, applying it to her face and neck regularly. The candle had burnt down to the wick and we sat in darkness, with only the light of the moon and the sparks from the dying fire to see her face by. She had not started screaming again, but her silence was almost as worrying. I had not wanted her to turn up dead on my property for fear of the gossip and scandal - but truth be told, after several hours with her this evening I wanted her to be all right far more strongly than I would have expected.

Suddenly she groaned, and clasped her hand to her head, her breathing became shallow. I froze, my hand halfway between the basin of cold water and her skin, and as her eyes fluttered open I saw confusion clouding them.

"Annelise?" I said, marvelling at how quickly it felt natural to say the first name of this girl I barely knew. Well, she was in bed, in a nightdress, and I was tending to her - I guessed I knew her a little.

She nodded her head, as if confirming that was who she was, and her eyes darted around the room.

"Let me light another candle," I said, desperate for something to do that might help things, and I found a spare candle on the chest and lit it in the fireplace. Shadows danced on the walls as I replaced the burnt-out candle in the holder, and then I looked back at the girl who had not yet uttered a word.

"Where am I?" she asked, and I wondered how far back I needed to go.

"Marvale House," I said, deciding to make things easy for her. "You fainted at dinner - I brought you up here to rest."

She groaned and closed her eyes, and I reached forward without thinking to touch her forehead and feel her temperature. Her eyes opened, but she did not say anything, and so I pressed my fingers against her skin. My heart dropped at the heat that was definitely still there.

"Do you-" There was a sharp rap on the door,

then Edith entered, followed by a man I presumed was the doctor.

"Lord Gifford," he said, nodding his head, and I reached out a hand to shake his. "And this is-"

"Annelise," I supplied. "She has a fever, and has been hallucinating, I think - although she seems a bit more lucid now."

The doctor nodded, and I stood to one side, letting him sit where I had been sat. She was still awake, although there was fear in her eyes now that had not been there a moment ago.

"How do you feel, Annelise?" the doctor asked loudly.

"H-hot," she said, although I saw her shiver. "And my head hurts."

He reached forward to touch her forehead, but she flinched away, something which she had not done when I had done the very same thing moments earlier.

"I need to see whether you have a fever," the doctor said, a little sharply. She let him that time, but I could see the difficulty she had with it, and when her eyes fluttered closed I moved to stand by her other side, feeling an overwhelming urge to protect her that I did not quite understand.

"Definitely a fever. You say she'd been out in

the rain?" he directed at Edith, who nodded. "Hard to say exactly what it is - I think we will need to see if the fever has broken by tomorrow, and if not she'll need to be bled."

"No!" she shrieked, as distressed as she had been hours earlier when I had found her staring at the ceiling. "No!" Her arms flailed and she reached out to grab my hand. I furled my fingers round hers without thinking, and knelt down beside her. I shushed her once more, hoping I was being soothing, not really understanding the sudden outburst.

"It's all right, Annelise. The doctor will make you better."

She shook her head, sobbing a little, squeezing my hand with surprising strength. "Please, no, I've seen what happens - my mother - I don't want-"

The doctor was looking irritated, but since he'd said the fever needed to be watched until morning, there was little more for him to do now. "Thank you, doctor," I said. "Is there anything else we should do tonight?"

He shook his head. "Plenty of rest, fluids, but don't let her get too cold. Keep the fire going and watch her for any signs of a fit."

I nodded, hoping desperately it did not come to that.

"I'll come again in the morning," he said, and Annelise whimpered but did not protest again.

"Thank you. Harris will pay you, if you go downstairs."

He tipped his hat and left the room, followed by Edith. I turned back to face Annelise, who still had hold of my hand, and was shaking.

"Come on," I said, encouraging her to lie down again. "There's no use getting so worked up about it all." She leant back into the pillows but did not let go of me. She pulled the blankets around herself with one hand, clearly cold despite the raging fever that was overtaking her body.

"Nicholas," she said, her eyes closed, and I could not help but smile.

"That's right."

"Please don't let him bleed me."

"You've got a nasty fever," I said, sitting down on the wooden floor beside the bed, bending my arm in an awkward fashion so she did not have to let go of my hand. "If the doctor thinks it is best..."

"They bled my mother," she said, pain in her voice. "So many times. And she became weaker, and weaker, and..."

She was clearly grieving, and I felt my heart tighten a little in a way I hadn't in a long time. She seemed so lost, ill in a strange house with so many fears. And she held on to me like I was the safe place, like I was the one who could protect her from all the evils this world had to offer.

I could protect her from one, I supposed. "I won't let him do it unless you say so, all right?" I said, and she gave a little smile and nodded.

"My head feels so heavy," she said, her lip trembling a little.

"Sleep," I said. "It will all feel better in the morning."

"I'm scared," she whispered. "I saw flames..."

"They weren't real," I reassured her. "You can sleep, you'll be safe. I'm not going anywhere."

Where had that promise come from? I had not planned to make it - no, I had envisaged her going back to sleep and me slipping back to my room, to finish that wine and get some rest myself.

But whatever complaints people might have had about me, I always kept my word - and so I would stay. I stretched my long legs and leant back against the wall, wondering if it were possible to get any sleep like this. When Edith reappeared to add to the fire, I simply gave her a smile, and wondered if she had slept a wink this night either.

Annelise rolled onto her side, facing me, but her eyes remained closed and her breathing constant, and for a moment I just watched her, finally looking untroubled in sleep. I wondered if I had ever been with someone in such a vulnerable moment. I had certainly never seen the woman I did not care to think about ill, or upset. My mother had always been very put together; perhaps before her death she had shown a little vulnerability, but I had been young and had not truly understood the severity of the situation.

It was an odd feeling, to be trusted so much, especially by someone who didn't even know my full name. And as I pondered what an odd turn this day had taken, my head leaning ever-so-slightly against her pillow, I drifted into sleep.

CHAPTER FIVE
Annelise

I was confused by so many things when I awoke the next morning. The first was the bed I was in, with its beautiful blue hangings. The second was the room I was in, with its intricately decorated ceiling and large fireplace. And the third - and possibly most confusing - was the man asleep on the floor next to me, holding my hand.

My breath quickened at the sight of him, and it wasn't just in panic. I remembered who he was, at least, even if I did not remember how I got to this room or why he was here. Nicholas, the lord of the manor, the man who had carried me in from the storm and invited me for dinner.

But why was he holding my hand?

My whole body ached and I tried to move a little, without waking him, but it was without success. His eyelids sprang open, revealing green eyes that I thought were the colour of emeralds, although I had never seen one up close.

He let go of my hand, and although I was relieved to be able to move my arm, I missed the warmth of it almost immediately.

"How are you feeling?" he asked, and memories of the previous night began to break through the haze in my mind.

"Everything aches," I admitted, wishing my mouth was not so dry.

"Can I?" he asked, the back of his fingertips hovering by my forehead, and I nodded without knowing what I was agreeing to. I wasn't sure if I was successful at concealing my gasp when his bare skin touch mine, but he smiled, and I tried to pretend it had not happened.

"Much better," he said. "You had a terrible fever, in the night," he said. "Do you remember?"

"Not really," I croaked. "Maybe some vague memories..."

He ran a hand through his dark hair, no less glorious for his night spent on the floor. "It didn't look good, for a while - but now it's broken..."

I struggled to get up. "Thank you," I said, suddenly realising I wore only a thin nightgown and pulling the blankets tightly around me. "I've taken advantage of your hospitality for far too long, though."

"What?" He looked at me for a moment, and I felt a blush rise to my cheeks. We were both dressed for bed, and although he had clearly slept on the floor, this was the first time I had ever shared a chamber with a man before. "You're not going anywhere."

"Excuse me?"

"The doctor wasn't sure you would make it through the night," he said, and I felt a sharp pain in my chest at the memory of a doctor and that terrible word: bleeding.

"Oh."

"And the weather is still terrible." He waved a hand to the window, where rain indeed poured down the window panes, and mist obscured the view. "There is no way you can go back out in that. You need to take a few days, rest, recuperate."

My eyes widened. A few days? I had come to find out about my mother, to spend a night at some local inn and then head back to London. Since Mother had died I took in washing like she had done, but I was up to date with it all and no-one would really miss me for a few days. I supposed I could make some inquiries, the inquiries I had failed to make last night...

But I was a servant's daughter. A washerwoman. How could I stay in this luxurious bed and recuperate in the house of a lord?

His voice gentled a little, and his eyes met mine. "It's no trouble," he said. "And you really need to make sure you are over the worst of it."

I nodded, feeling powerless when he spoke with such care in his voice.

"Excellent. Well." He cleared his throat and ran a hand through his hair again. "I'm going to make myself presentable, have some food brought up here and while we break our fast, you can tell me the real reason for your visit. Is that acceptable?"

I nodded, knowing this was inevitable, but also knowing I would not reveal everything to him if I could help it.

He left, and I lay back on the pillows, realising how exhausted I truly was. Perhaps he was right; perhaps I did need to rest. The last thing I needed was to end up in the same state as Mother had. There would be no-one to look after me if I were sick for months, that was for sure.

As I closed my eyes for a few minutes, I realised I hadn't asked him the most important question - and I doubted I would have the bravery to ask now: why had he stayed the night beside me?

CHAPTER SIX

Nicholas

Bread and cheese were brought up, along with some spiced wine to chase away the chill of the morning, and I made myself comfortable on a chair by the fire, while she remained in bed. Her cheeks were still flushed, but I was struck by how beautiful she was. A true natural beauty; even ill, even in a poorly-fitting nightgown, even looking uncomfortable in someone else's home.

I pushed the thought from my mind. Beautiful or not, she had no business in my head.

"So," I said, after she had taken a few bites of the manchet bread and sipped the wine. "Can you tell me why you're here?"

She nodded. Her voice was soft, and it sounded like it took a lot of effort to speak loudly enough for me to hear - but I needed to know this.

"My mother had a link with Marvale - she was travelling back here when she..." She paused, taking a deep breath, her cheeks flushing deeper red at the effort. "When she passed away. I wanted to know why she had tried to travel all the way here, when she was already weak and frail."

"I'm sorry for your loss," I said, an automatic reaction. How many times had I heard those words after the death of my father? And yet rarely had they sounded sincere. So often there was an undertone of 'but at least you have the lordship now'. And that hadn't been how I'd felt - it still wasn't how I felt. Perhaps I was unusual among the titled folk, but I had no desire for this name that had been thrust upon me after my father's death.

Her eyes lowered a little and it looked like she was holding back tears. I was relieved when she looked at me again and her eyes were dry; there was something about crying women that made me forget to be guarded.

"Thank you," she said. "So I was hoping to find that out... and then I got caught in that terrible storm."

She sneezed three times in a row, and I wished I could feel her forehead and see if the raging fever had returned. But I was on the other side of the room now, and the closeness we had shared last night seemed wholly inappropriate in the cold light of day.

Thankfully, a knock announcing the arrival

of the doctor saved me from embarrassing myself and jumping to her aid - although her face went white when he appeared and I remembered her fears from the night before.

"Good morning, Miss-"

"Edwards."

"You seem better today. Let me-"

He reached over and touched her head, as I had imagined myself doing, and grimaced a little.

"Still a fever, although certainly not as severe as last night, and you are clearly more lucid. I would still recommend a blood-letting-"

"No." She was forceful, rather than hysterical, this time, and she looked at me for confirmation that this would not be happening. I nodded, and although the doctor seemed irritated he said nothing more on the matter.

"Plenty of rest, do not let her get cold, and some nourishing food. If the fever returns as badly as last night, call me."

I nodded, and then he was gone, and it was just the two of us again.

And it seemed we would be remaining together at Marvale a little while longer, if the doctor's orders were to be followed.

CHAPTER SEVEN
Annelise

"Perhaps I could leave this evening," I said, fiddling with the cover over my legs. To have been in this house at all had felt like a dream, but now to be stuck here and a burden upon this Adonis of a man was turning into a nightmare.

"The last time you tried to leave you collapsed in my hallway," he said, and I blushed. "No. You need to rest and make sure that fever's gone before you think of leaving."

"I don't want to be a burden - more of a burden than I already have been," I admitted.

He waved his hand in the air as though it were nothing. "It's of no consequence," he said. "You can borrow more of my sister's clothes, if you need to."

"Thank you," I said, feeling a wave of gratitude at this seemingly brusque man who showed surprising care in the face of my inconvenient illness.

"Besides," he said, a grin on his face that I had not yet seen, but which reminded me of a naughty school boy. "I do like to solve a mystery. Perhaps we can figure out your mother's reason to visit here together."

I tried to smile, but I very much hoped he would not find out the full truth. I knew I should not be ashamed of my upbringing, but here, surrounded by this opulence, and with the misunderstanding of my status already out there, it was hard to imagine admitting I was the daughter of a servant who had once served under this very roof.

CHAPTER EIGHT
Nicholas

She slept most of that afternoon, and when I peeked round the door before dinner - telling myself it was the least I could do when she had become so ill on my property - she was still fast asleep, and so I took my dinner alone in the library, looking over some of the accounts while I did so. I'd asked cook to send her up a nourishing stew, per the doctor's orders, and so I had the same with a hunk of bread and a large tankard of ale. The weather was still pretty miserable, although not quite as terrible as the day before had been. I supposed it was fairly standard for late February, but being stuck inside without the opportunity to ride out always made me a little irritated.

The books, as I knew from a previous perusal, showed the estate was not in good shape. Once upon a time, Father had been a competent and keen landlord, but in later years his mind had not been what it was and I was ashamed to admit that I had not stepped in to help. I had not thought he was struggling as much as my sister had claimed... but unfortunately the accounts before me suggested things were worse than either of us could have imagined.

I sighed, and closed the pages as I finished off the ale. Staring at the numbers wouldn't do any good; I needed to have a plan. Not only was the house in need of repairs and modernisation, the whole village needed work. And if we were to pay for it, the farmland needed to be more productive than it was. I knew I needed to meet with the men who knew this land well, who could advise me - but it was hard to admit I needed advice, and even harder to know who I could trust to dole it out.

Not for the first time that week, I wished my Father was around to give some much-needed guidance.

CHAPTER NINE

Annelise

It was dark outside when I next became aware of the room I was in, and I was pleased to find my head did not seem to ache like it had before. A candle had been lit on the far side of the room, casting shadows along with the fireplace that danced across the wooden floors.

I did not know how long I had slept, but when I sat up my mouth was dry and my limbs tingled from a lack of use. On a tray beside the bed was what looked like a stew, and a glass of spiced wine that was still a little warm. I drank and ate heartily, feeling like my appetite was a good sign that my body was recovering from whatever had befallen it. Not that anyone would really have known, had I died here in this fine house from a fever. I had no mother, knew not who or where my father was, and I had moved around so many times that friends were scarce indeed.

It was with those morose thoughts that I fell asleep once more, full of food and wine and an unfortunate dose of misery. As my eyelids fluttered closed I allowed myself one small moment to wish he had dined with me, to wish we could have conversed about anything, that he could have distracted me from the unhappiness inside my mind.

And then I was asleep once more, with only my dreams to keep me company.

◆ ◆ ◆

"Good morning, miss," a quiet voice said as I blinked into the early morning sun which streamed through a gap in the curtains. At least that must mean the rain had taken a break from falling, and perhaps would mean I could leave this place and my disastrous mission.

"Good morning," I croaked, reaching for a drink that was once again beside me.

"How are you feeling?" she asked, as she remade the fire and swept away the ashes.

"Better, I think," I said. "If it's not too much trouble, I should like to wash my face."

"'Course not, miss," she said, a grin on her young face. "His lordship has told us to bring you anything you require."

"That's very kind of him," I said, wishing I could ask where Nicholas was, why I had not seen him since the morning before. Of course, there was no reason I should ever see him again - but that thought was far more unpleasant to me than I thought it should be.

And then he was there, standing in the doorway, a smile on his lips that had me mesmerised. What was it about this man that made my eyes unwilling to be dragged away?

"Good morning, Miss Edwards," he said, and I tried to remember when I had given him my last name. I so liked to hear 'Annelise' falling from his lips. "I'm glad to see you looking so well."

I dipped my head, knowing this extended time spent in bed was not going to help my pale complexion or unruly hair, and merely thanked him.

"If you wish to join me for lunch," he said, "You could borrow another dress. And we could discuss what I have discovered about your mother."

My eyes darted up at that, but his features were relaxed and showed no sign of irritation, so I did not think he could have found the truth. Besides, other than my surname, I did not think I had given him anything he could use in his investigation!

"That would be lovely, thank you, my lord," I found myself saying, even though in truth I felt a rising panic and a desire to run from the house.

But I needed to know what he knew - and I had not wholly forgotten my reason for this ill-fated visit. I still planned to visit the local village and ask around - and perhaps whatever he had found out would save me some time.

My savings would not last long, and I needed to be home and taking in washing once more if I were to be able to pay next month's rent on my own.

I so wished I did not have to be on my own.

CHAPTER TEN
Nicholas

I waited in the great hall, not sure whether she would actually join me or not. She had looked much better than she had done the night before, and she needed to eat - so I hoped I was not contradicting the doctor's orders by inviting her to lunch.

She entered in another dress of my sister's, green this time and with intricate white braiding. I never paid much attention to fashions, and had no idea how old this dress was, but it certainly suited Annelise. I found myself smiling when her eyes met mine, and reminded myself that I was merely being hospitable to a young lady who had fallen ill.

"How are you feeling?" I asked as she sat.

"Tired," she admitted, "But much better, thank you."

"I hope you feel well enough to eat?"

She nodded, then blushed. "And I'm intrigued as to what information you have found out, since I gave you so little myself!"

I could not stop my grin at that. I ran a hand through my hair and waited to answer until two bowls of steaming soup had been placed in front of us.

"I dug out the books containing the names of those who have lived and worked in the area over the last decade," I said, pleased to see she was eating the soup. "And there are three women with the surname Edwards who had lived here in the time period you are talking about. There are marriage records, addresses, and birth records - which I thought might be of use."

She smiled, but did not seem overwhelmed by my discovery. I wondered if it was all information she knew already - or whether there was more to this search she was letting on.

"Thank you," she said. "Perhaps I could see the records, later?"

I nodded. "Of course. And if you can give more information, I'll happily ask the staff and tenants if they might know your mother's reason for visiting the area."

Her breath seemed to catch in her throat, and as she pressed her eyes closed for a second I wondered if she were taking a turn for the worse. When her eyes reopened, however, I realised she was battling emotions about her mother that she did not wish to share, and so I focussed for a few moments on eating the soup before me. It was delicious, as cook's meals tended to be, and warmed me through on this chilly February day.

"Where do you live, when you are not catching cold by lakes?" I asked with a gentle smile when she seemed to have regained control of her feelings.

She laughed softly at that. "London," she said, without being specific. "And do you live here all year?"

"I haven't in a long time," I said, tearing off a chunk of bread. "But... I need to focus on Marvale, and the estate, and the tenants for now. Things have been left alone for too long."

She nodded, but had nothing more to say on the subject, and for a few moments we slipped into companionable silence.

CHAPTER ELEVEN

Annelise

He did not enquire any further as to my station in life nor my profession, and for that I was pleased. I did not want to have to lie to this man who had behaved so kindly to me - but I certainly could not tell him the truth. I already felt like an impostor, sat here in this beautiful dress, eating delicious food in a home that he considered needed updating.

What would he think of my life in a two-roomed home in London, taking in other people's washing to make a living? I did not like to be embarrassed of my circumstances, but being here did not make me want to publicise them.

"Where is your sister now?" I asked when the silence dragged on a little too long. He had offered me her clothes, and I presumed they were ones she no longer used - and I certainly had not seen her in the house.

"Married," he said. "Moved away up North two years ago. She was living here still, before then - hence why half her wardrobe still appears to be here!"

I laughed, as though I understood leaving behind expensive dresses. Presumably she had bought more, or had them bought for her - either way, what I was wearing was no longer of use to her.

"It must be lonely, living here alone," I said, before I realised the words had left my mouth. I realised how it sounded; like I was angling for information about a possible marriage - or, heaven forbid, a proposal. It was just hard for me, having spent my whole life in small dwellings with my mother, to imagine living alone in such a grand house. I felt my cheeks redden and looked back to my food. "Forgive me if I have overstepped."

"It's fine, Annelise," he said, and my whole body warmed to the sound of my name on his lips. My eyes met his and he smiled, then shrugged. "As I said, I've been at court a lot in recent years, and court is never quiet." He chuckled, and I wished I knew a little of the world he spoke of. I had seen the King and Queen as they paraded through London, or down the Thames - but I had no knowledge of life at court that did not come from hearsay. "And when I would come back here... well, before I was Lord, my family were here. And now..."

His gaze moved to a portrait on the wall, and I could not help but follow his eyes as I looked upon an image of a father, mother and two small children. I presumed the boy with raven hair was him, although it must have been from many years ago.

I gave him a moment, as he had done for me, but instead of moving on I could not help but ask; "And your mother?"

"She passed away many years ago," he said with a sigh. "It's just me and Mary left."

"I'm sorry. Losing a parent is something almost everyone must face, and yet that does not seem to make it any easier."

He met my eyes, and I felt a shock as though he were seeing into my very heart. "Wise words," he said, seemingly unaffected by whatever had just passed between us, and I took a deep breath and reminded myself I was recovering from a serious fever that had made me hallucinate.

I could not possibly have feelings for this lord.

For Nicholas.

CHAPTER TWELVE
Nicholas

When she spoke of the pain of losing a parent, it took everything in my willpower not to let her see how much her words affected me. Why they did, I could not say, but in that moment I felt that no-one had ever truly understood my feelings as well as Annelise Edwards.

I knew she wanted to know why I was not married, or whether I had plans to - it was the logical conclusion from her question. But I could not bring myself to talk about *her*, to reveal the fact that I had been jilted to someone who was wonderfully unaware of the fact. And I could not say I did not believe I would ever trust a woman again because - well, because that was not something you said in polite conversation with a woman you barely knew.

She was obviously unwed, and if my deductions were correct was not titled. I did not know if she came from any money or none, and in truth I did not care - but she wore Mary's dress so well, and had impeccable table manners, so I was inclined to think she had some wealth in her family.

But now it seemed she was all alone, and I knew as well as she did that money made no difference to loneliness, or grief, or heartbreak.

If it did, I should not have been suffering from all three.

CHAPTER THIRTEEN
Annelise

"Are you feeling all right?" he asked me, and I could feel bright spots dancing on my cheeks. I felt a little tired, a little achy, but not ready to go back to the bedchamber yet. Lunch sat warmly in my stomach, topped up with the spiced wine that seemed to be served in abundance, and I was enjoying the conversation that I had not had a chance to enjoy in several months.

Who knew conversation would be so missed when one lived alone?

"Yes, thank you." I wondered if he mistook my rosy cheeks for fever, but I didn't feel feverish. I felt excited without reason, and I did not want this pleasant afternoon to end.

"Would you care for a game of chess? Since the weather is still so terrible, I am stuck indoors anyway."

I blushed, wondering how to politely decline, before deciding on the truth. "That sounds lovely, my lord-"

"Nicholas."

His correction made my breath catch in my throat, and it took me a second to get back to my train of thought.

"Nicholas," I said, his name heavy on my tongue. "It would be lovely - but I'm afraid I've never learnt to play." Perhaps that would make my status abundantly clear - but he just smiled in that way that made everything around us cease to exist.

"I can teach you."

And somehow I was agreeing, and following him from the room.

CHAPTER FOURTEEN
Nicholas

What possessed me to extend the time I was spending with her - especially when she was supposed to be resting - I did not know, but the suggestion of chess was in the air between us before I'd even considered the words, and her charming admission that she didn't know how to play had only made me want to share the moment with her more.

It was dangerous to question my thinking, when I had so recently been burnt by a woman, and so I put any queries from my mind. By tomorrow, perhaps the day after at the latest, she would be gone, and I would have plenty of time and silence to focus on the matters that needed to be taken in hand. For now, I would simply enjoy having someone to dine with, converse with, laugh with - and not read anything into it.

CHAPTER FIFTEEN
Annelise

The rules seemed fairly simple, although I was sure he would have to remind me as we went along, and as we sat in front of the fireplace, playing with the marble chess set that probably cost more than my rent for a year, it felt like I was in a dream. This was a room I had not yet seen, clearly set up for cards, chess, pianoforte playing - but it still felt cosy, and although I could see some parts of the walls and windows that needed attention, it certainly wasn't in the dire condition his earlier words had suggested.

I considered my moves carefully, thrilled when it seemed like he had to think about his moves instead of easily winning, but it didn't take long before he paused and - with a look of apology on his face - said 'check'.

I grinned; I didn't mind losing, it was fun to

play, and the fact that he had not won in minutes made me happy. Still I managed to evade him a little longer, and when the inevitable check mate came I felt a flutter in my heart and a smile on my lips.

"Thank you, my- Nicholas." My Nicholas? That certainly was not how it was meant to come out, but he did not seem to react and I hoped my blush was hidden by the flickering light from the fire's flames. "I enjoyed that."

"Another round?" he asked, a glint in his eye and a smile on his face that I could not resist.

"All right," I said, reaching for my glass of wine. My head felt a little like a spinning plate at the circus, and I wondered if it was the wine, or my proximity to this handsome man, that was making me feel so giddy. I blinked my eyes once, twice, but the feeling did not go. "I think I just need to-" I planned to get some air in the corridor, but I did not make it that far. My knees buckled but, before I hit the ground, Nicholas's strong arms were around me. I leant against his broad chest, revelling in the strength of his body as it stopped me falling, and took several deep breaths.

"Are you all right?" he asked, his voice soft and so close to my ear.

I nodded; "Sorry. I just felt so dizzy..."

"I overtaxed you this evening," he said. "My

apologies - I should have let you rest."

I tried to smile, which was made even more difficult by the feel of his heart beneath my hand as it rested on his chest. I had marvelled at the feel of his body when he had carried me in from the rain, and the feel of him beneath my fingertips now made me want to swoon all over again.

"It's not your fault," I murmured. "But I perhaps I should retire."

He nodded, and then before I could say a word he had swept me into his arms.

"Nicholas!" I said, shock colouring my voice, but he merely grinned and strode towards the door.

"I will not have you collapsing in my hallway again," he said. "Allow me to deliver you safely to your bedchamber."

I blushed, but argued no more, and savoured the feeling of being held tight in his warm arms. It was something I might never know again, and so for now I stayed quiet and let the sensation overwhelm me.

He climbed the stairs with little difficulty, despite my added weight, and as woozy as my head felt, I could not feel sad at my predicament. For a society lady, this would surely mean ruin - but no-one cared about my name, nor my reputation, and when would I ever be in such a fine house, with such a fine man holding me again?

Almost certainly never.

He laid me on the bed as if I weighed as much as the feathers in the mattress, and I felt myself blush at his eyes on me.

"I'm sorry," I said, already missing the warmth of his chest against my body. The fire was burning, but somehow it did not have the same effect. "I did not mean to ruin our evening."

He smiled then, a smile that could so easily break a heart. "You did not ruin it," he said, and I felt my heart soar. This was dangerous territory, to covet this man's smiles and words and time when I should have left the day I arrived. "How do you feel now?"

"Tired," I admitted, wondering how it was possible to feel so tired when I had done no manual labour in days. "But not as ill as the other night."

"Good. I shall call for the doctor if you wish me to..."

I shook my head vehemently. "No. No, thank you."

He smiled again then, a knowing smile as if he understood me, and I felt that there was a good chance he did.

"I shall have some supper brought up to you," he said. "No more breaking the doctor's orders!"

I sighed, but knew he was right, and as soon as the door closed behind him my eyes fluttered closed.

CHAPTER SIXTEEN

Nicholas

It seemed totally natural, when I asked for a plate of breakfast to be sent up to Annelise, to follow it up with my own plate and sit on a chair by the fire, chatting with her as we broke our fast. I knew it was not a good plan, to get used to someone being here - although, I supposed I must marry one day, even if it were just to beget an heir. I would not wish to dishonour my father by letting Marvale fall out of our hands and into those of some distant cousin, as would surely occur if I sired no male heir.

But I had sworn off love when my heart had been broken, and so I knew such a marriage would only be for convenience. Would such a marriage allow easy breakfasts and laughter over games of chess? I could not quite imagine it to be so. In fact, when I imagined myself married, these days I imagined separate households, especially once children had been conceived. A lonely life, but one at least that would not cause any further heartbreak.

"I must ride out, this afternoon," I said, knowing it was safer to keep some distance between me and my unexpected house guest. "To see some tenant farmers. I will inquire using your mother's name, if you like."

She smiled then, and I wondered what lengths I would go to in order to see that grateful smile once more. It warmed me like the sun we were so sorely lacking, and made my thoughts feel so much less sharp and angry.

"Thank you," she said. "I would appreciate it."

She did not seem to wish to linger on the topic of her mother, despite it being the reason she had come here, and I wondered if the loss was still too painful.

"Do you live alone, in London?" I asked, not sure where the thought had come from, and her wide eyes at the question made me regret asking it. She was hiding something, I was sure of it - another reason to never trust a woman.

And then she nodded, and although it seemed like she did not want to part with the information, she did anyway.

"Since my mother died... yes, I have lived

alone." She sighed. "I hate it."

The admission melted something inside of me, some wall that had been allowing me to pretend that living in this home that had been full of family, and love, simply as a single man, was easy to do.

Yes, I was surrounded by servants, but it was not the same. I could not relax with them, nor they with me, like I could my family. It just was not the done thing - and I would never put them in that position.

"I had not lived with my father for a long time, when he died," I said, the words finding their way from my mouth without effort or thought. "I lived at court, I travelled, I attended house parties, I-" I paused, wondering how much I really wanted to admit to some girl from London who I knew next to nothing about.

I glanced at her, sat in her borrowed nightrail and robe, her eyes open, her mouth soft, her hands palm up and relaxed, just waiting to hear whatever I wanted to share. And the months of grief and loneliness and goddamn silence came crashing down around me, and I spoke words that no-one else had heard, that no-one else could possibly know.

"I am so full of regrets. That I did not spend more time with him, when he was alive. That I did not come back to help, when my sister suggested I should. That I did not realise-"

My voice broke then, and I looked away into the fire, not willing to let her see the tears that were threatening to fall. I had not cried over my father's death when it had happened - I certainly was not going to do it now, in company.

And then those soft hands were somehow on mine, and she was kneeling before me, holding my hands as though it were the most natural thing in the world.

"Oh, Nicholas," she said, and the care in her voice broke my last ounce of control, although I kept my face to the fire as the tears fell. "I'm sure he knew you loved him. I'm sure he was proud of the man you had become, that you were out in the world on your own."

The words made my chest feel tight, and I focussed on the feel of her hands on mine, of her presence beside me, as I struggled to regain control.

"When Mother and I would speak of me being married one day, and leaving her, she told me that as much as it would pain her to say goodbye, she would always be grateful that I was healthy and happy and able to live a life apart from her. And I'm sure that's what all parents think."

How could she say words like that, words

that gave me hope that my father had not been disappointed in his son and heir, when she had never known him, when she barely knew me?

I turned my head, knowing tears still lay in my eyes but needing to see her. As my eyes met hers, something roared inside me, some feeling I had never known before.

It was not the lust I had felt about women in the past, even about the woman I was going to make my wife. It was a desire to protect, to unite, to close the door and shut out the rest of the world. Her hands stayed on mine but by the little gasp she made I knew she felt the change, felt the intense energy in the room. Her lips, that had so recently spoken such wonderful words, had dropped open, and I could think of nothing but kissing them, of showing her how her words had affected me.

And then there was a knock on the door, and she jumped away from me so fast I was afraid she might fall. My eyes widened and as a serving girl came in to collect our plates, seemingly unaware of what she had interrupted, I practically flew through the door, spitting out my excuses as I did so.

The interruption had cleared my head, and I realised what I had been about to do. Something I had never done - taking advantage of an innocent woman who was in my home, who was under my protection.

And worst of all, I had nearly let myself open up to someone once more. I had made that vow mere months ago, and yet here I was: the first sign of a pretty woman who seemed to care and I would throw away the pain and hurt of being jilted by another.

What an idiot I was.

CHAPTER SEVENTEEN
Annelise

I could hardly catch my breath as I settled myself back onto the bed. The serving girl left as quickly as she'd appeared, not aware of what she had broken up.

And what was that, exactly? Nicholas had fled the room as soon as we were discovered, and my heart was racing faster than I had thought possible - but had anything actually happened?

I had held his hands. I hadn't meant to, certainly hadn't planned it, but when he'd spoken with such anguish in his voice... I could not help it. Did we not all have regrets when it came to our parents? I wished I had stopped Mother travelling to Marvale when she was clearly not well enough to do so - but I had not. I wished I'd told her before she left how much I loved her, how much I needed her, how empty and quiet my life would be without her.

But I hadn't. I had said goodbye, hugged her - but in truth I was annoyed that she was going when I didn't think it was a good idea.

And now I would never be able to tell her all the things that I wished I had.

Tears were streaming down my face now, and despite being in the warmest, biggest, most comfortable bedroom I had ever been in, I felt a longing for my own little bed in our small home, that was filled with the memories of my mother.

CHAPTER EIGHTEEN
Nicholas

I rode hard and fast, arriving at my destination while my thoughts were still in that bedroom. The tenant farmers had a lot they needed to talk to me about, and I knew that improving their output was key to making Marvale more profitable once more. If only my mind could remain focussed on the words they were saying...

"My lord?"

I had obviously missed something important, and the young man in front of me waited for an answer I did not have. I gave myself a mental shake, feeling embarrassed. There were far greater issues in the world than whether or not I had wanted to kiss Annelise - and I needed to focus my mind on them.

"My apologies," I said, hoping my sincerity

was clear. "Could you repeat the last part?"

He smiled, and happily continued. "As I was saying, we need better irrigation, and more men if we're to have the kind of harvests we used to."

"And that all needs money," I said with a grimace.

"It does, my lord."

"I will see what I can do," I said. "I must speak with the ironmonger too, and see if we can make more of the mining available in the area."

He nodded. "That seems a sound idea, my lord. Marvale is perfectly capable of being self-sufficient."

It just hadn't been in recent years - although that was something I did not voice. "Thank you for your time. We will make this work - I will make sure of it." I had the money to invest, but I knew if I spent every penny and the estate could not provide for itself, I could not support it indefinitely. A plan was needed - a plan I was trying very hard to come up with.

"Thank you, my lord," he said, with a tip of his cap, but before we parted ways I decided to try my luck.

"Can I ask - do you know of an Elise Edwards from this area?"

He thought for a moment, before shaking his head. "My ma might, though," he said. "She's known everyone round here. She's up at the house - shall I run and ask her?"

"If it's not too much trouble," I said, hope growing at the idea that it might be so easy to discover someone who knew Annelise's mother, and therefore might know her reason for returning. "I'll walk with you, if that's acceptable?"

He nodded, and we talked of the sheep in the nearby field, and of how nice it was to get a break in the rain.

His home was modest but inviting, with a fire burning in the hearth and the sound of children laughing nearby. I did not know if they were his children, or merely younger siblings, but the sound gave it a homely feel that I had not known in a long time.

I stayed outside, not wishing to intrude, but heard him through the window as clearly as if he had been stood next to me.

"Ma? Do you know of an Elise Edwards?"

"Ay."

My heart jumped - but no more seemed to be forthcoming. Instead, the young man appeared in the doorway. "Would you like to come in? My mother says she knows of the lady."

I thanked him as I stepped into the warm room, full of the smell of smoke from the fire and something cooking in a pot above it.

The lady tried to stand, but I shook my head, perching on a bench before she had a chance.

"Thank you for your time," I said, before she could speak. "I believe you have heard of the lady I speak of?"

She coughed twice, and her voice was weak when she spoke. "Yes, my lord," she said. "She lived round here for a long time - worked in Marvale a spell, too."

I was a little shocked at that knowledge, although I had gathered Annelise probably did not come from great money. I filed it away, letting the woman continue. "She was always great friends with the gardener - Mr Stockwall, I believe his name is. Still gardens at Marvale, or so I'm told." She coughed once more. "Don't get out much these days."

"He does," I said, with a smile. "Thank you, madam, you have been most helpful."

"She was a sweet young thing, when she worked here. Disappeared in a flurry though, if I remember correctly. Wonder what became of her..."

"I'm afraid I have heard she passed away recently."

She sighed and leaned back in her rickety chair. "Ah dear. Time gets to all of us, in the end. I was sorry to hear about your father, too, my lord."

The rawness of this morning's conversation was still beating away in my chest and I felt emotion bubbling up to the surface. "Thank you, madam. It was a hard blow to us all." I swallowed, willing myself to not look a fool, and then stood. "I must be on my way now - but I thank you both, for your time and information. Good day."

I let my mind wander as I rode back to the house. Should I speak with Stockwall myself? Or give the information to Annelise, to do with as she wished? Her mother had worked at Marvale, it seemed - in what capacity, I did not know - and perhaps she did not want me knowing that fact. Not that I cared - I had not asked her background and she had told no lies, not that I knew of anyway. But perhaps I should let her do any further digging.

It also seemed prudent, I thought, as I felt my horse speed up between my thighs, reacting to the nervous energy I felt pouring out from skin, to distance myself a little. I had stopped - or should I say, had been stopped, - in time today. I was under no illusion that I would have kissed Annelise if I had been left alone with her any longer - and that would have been no good for anyone.

No good at all.

CHAPTER NINETEEN

Annelise

There was a knock on the door, a clearing of a throat, and then the slow swing open. "May I come in?"

My heart raced at his very voice, and I tried to school my expression to be one of calmness and serenity. "Of course," I said, a smile playing on my lips without permission.

Would he mention this morning? Or were we to forget it had ever happened?"

"How are you feeling?" he asked, although surely the fact that I was sat up in a chair, dressed and reading a book suggested the answer?

"Much better, my lord," I said.

"That is wonderful to hear." Wonderful because it meant I could leave soon? I presumed so, although nothing in his countenance suggested that to be the case. But how could his feelings be anything other than that?

He looked awkward as he took a seat by the fire, noticeably leaving the door wide open, despite the draught it let in. I wished the easiness of our conversation from this morning had not flitted away. "I have a lead," he said, looking at me but seeming to be avoiding my gaze at the same time. "About your mother."

"Oh?" Panic pooled in my chest; he must know I was the daughter of a servant, that I had hidden my background from him, that I was not made to wear dresses such as these.

"A name, that is all - of someone who she used to be friends with. Someone who works here, as luck would have it. Mr Stockwall, the gardener. I am happy to speak with him, on your behalf, but I thought I would see if you want to do so, yourself."

Relief washed over me as no accusations were hurled in my direction, and gratitude that he had left the conversation with the gardener to me. Perhaps this friend would know why Mother had felt the need to travel when she was so weak. Perhaps he would have the answers...

Or perhaps this was all as good as a wild goose chase.

"Thank you," I said, his eyes finally meeting mine and sending a blush across my cheeks for no obvious reason. "I would like to speak with him myself. Perhaps this afternoon, if you don't mind me distracting him from his duties."

He smiled; "Of course not. I just hope you can find the answers you are looking for."

"Thank you. Nicholas." I could not stop myself; I needed him to know how much I appreciated his efforts, and his name seemed like the only way I could show him he had affected me. Oh how he had affected me, that smile, that laugh, those eyes...

"My pleasure...Annelise."

I was a fool. And yet it felt so wonderful to be fooled, just for now. To fool myself into believing the looks he gave me, into thinking that somewhere in my future there could be a marriage to a man like Nicholas. Someone to fill my days and nights with conversation and laughter and warmth. Someone who would take care of me, and who I could take care of in return.

When I was working every hour the sun gave us, there was no time to daydream of love and marriage and children, but as I recuperated in this sumptuous bedroom, there was plenty of time to imagine a very different sort of life.

And as much as I knew I would be sad to leave and give up on the daydream, at least I could enjoy the pretence for now. And if Mr Stockwall had answers - well, then my trip had most definitely not been in vain.

*   *   *

I cleared my throat as I approached the old man weeding in what look like a rose bed. He looked up, an easy smile on his face, and I could not help but smile back.

"Mr Stockwall?" I asked, and he nodded.

"Aye, but you can call me Rupert, lass. What can I do to help ye?"

I could not quite place his accent, although I thought it could be Scottish, but now did not seem the time to ask. "I'm Annelise," I said, as he stood and doffed his cap. It took me a moment to remember the fancy dress I was in, and the image he must have of me. "Annelise Edwards."

I watched him closely to see if the name triggered any sort of response, but it did not appear to - and so I delved further. "I've come to Marvale to find out why my mother wished to return - and I was hoping you could help me." I glanced behind him and saw a stone bench, built into the wall. "Could we sit?"

He looked confused, but followed me without argument.

"My mother," I said, once we were sat on the

cold stone, "Was called Elise. Elise Edwards."

I saw shock register on his face, and then he swallowed as though he were choking on the words or, even just the air. Finally, he spat out: "Was?"

With a gasp that I could not control, I realised that he had no idea of her passing - and that, once again, I would have to discuss it whilst trying not to cry.

I looked down at my skirts, green today, and fiddled with a loose thread as I spoke. "She passed away," I said. "Last year."

"Oh. Oh... I am so sorry to hear that." I could tell his words were true; the emotion in them could not be a lie.

"She was... she was travelling here, in fact," I whispered, tears welling in my own eyes. "And I just... I needed to know why she came back. Why she travelled, when she was already so ill and weak. Why..." I took a deep breath, shocked that I was divulging quite so much to yet another man I barely knew. "Why she left me to come here, at the end."

And then he was sobbing, and I had no idea what to do.

I reached across to pat his arm, a little awkwardly, and thankfully it only took a few moments for him to regain control of his emotions.

"I'm sorry," he said, taking a few deep breaths. "I- I- I'm not really sure how to say this."

His words caused an anxious knot to build in my stomach, and I wondered if chasing this mystery had been a mistake. "Please, just tell me," I said, and whether he needed to get the words off his chest or just heard some desperation in my voice, I did not know, but he began to speak.

"I wrote to your mother, last year," he said turning his cap over and over in his hands. "Telling her I was dying."

My mouth formed a silent gasp, but he shook his head before I can speak.

"It's all right - they think they were wrong, now, the doctors. But for a while I believed I was dying, and I wrote to your mother - to say goodbye." He took a ragged breath, and looked at my face for a moment before returning his gaze to the floor. "And if she was insistent on coming here, even if she was not well enough... well, I'm guessing that's why."

I nodded, feeling a little dazed at the fact that I had actually found an answer to the question that had been haunting me since the news of my mother's death. But somehow, it didn't feel like the whole story. Questions still burned to be answered, questions such as-

"Why?" I realised it was rude as soon as I'd said it, but the word left my mouth before I had given it a second thought. I blushed, and tried to rephrase in a way that would not hurt his feelings. "I'm sorry. That sounds terribly blunt but... why would she risk her own life, to say goodbye?"

A sad smile crinkled his mouth and eyes, and for a moment I thought he would not answer me. When he did, his words were not what I was expecting to hear.

"We were in love," he said, without fanfare, as though that was the sort of thing one heard about one's mother every day. "Back then... back when she lived here, when she worked here. We were in love - and I suppose she never forgot that."

It took me a moment to process his words. They were in love - but why, then, had my mother left this place? Why hadn't she married this man, who seemed perfectly pleasant, and chosen the life she led instead? She obviously had not married my father, either - did she not care for marriage?

And then, as my head began to spin a little from the myriad of thoughts swirling around inside it, a sudden thought blossomed from the whirling mess. Could they, in fact, be one and the same?

That was a thought for another time.

"Why..." I began, framing my words carefully, sure I was overstepping propriety but hoping he would not mind. "Why did she leave, then?"

He sighed, and rubbed a hand down his leg, as though trying to warm it up. I hadn't noticed the drop in temperature, my head being wholly focussed on these revelations, but now I realised it was certainly getting colder again. I wished I'd borrowed a cloak, too, instead of just a dress - I certainly could not afford to become ill again.

"I can't honestly tell you, lass. I can say..." He paused to bite his lip. "I was betrothed, to a local girl. We'd been promised for a long time - before I even knew your mother - but once Elise and I realised how we felt, I planned to break it off the next time I saw her."

"And then she just left. One day she was here, working, and the next she was gone. She left me a note, wishing me well and saying she was going to London, and to have a happy life."

It was all too much to take in. I closed my eyes for a moment and tried to focus on my breathing, letting the questions go for just a minute. I had my answers - or at least some of them - but what I was not expecting was to end up with more questions than I had arrived with.

When I opened my eyes he was waiting and watching with a serious look on his face. "Are you all right, lass?" he asked, and I nodded reflexively.

"I think so," I said. "It's just a lot to think about. I thought... I thought I knew my mother well, but it seems perhaps I did not."

He nodded, as though he understood. "You look a lot like her," he said, and I could not help but smile.

"You think?"

He nodded. "Her eyes, and your mannerisms are so alike." He smiled wistfully. "I'm so sorry I caused her to travel. And I'm so sorry I didn't get a chance to say goodbye."

"She was dying," I said, managing to get the words out before tears built up in my eyes. "Before she left. We both knew it, although she wasn't very keen on the doctors visiting. If she'd written you a letter, perhaps she would have saved us all a lot of trouble!"

He gave a hollow laugh. "Elise always liked to say things in person, though. That's why I was so surprised, when she left and wrote me a letter. It wasn't her style."

"Did you marry the other woman?" I asked, curiosity getting the better of me.

He nodded. "Not for a long time after. I was broken-hearted, to tell you the truth. But when

I explained it all to Betsie, she understood more than I would have ever expected. And after a few years... well, we had grown much closer."

"I'm glad you found someone," I said, thinking of all those years where it was just my mother and me. She had always said she was a widow, although I had known from a young age that wasn't true. It was just what you said, so no-one asked awkward questions about the father of your child.

And I had asked... and I had been told very few details. She told me she had loved him, and that he hadn't been able to stay with her. And that was all I knew.

And the thought that this could be him, before me now - well, that was too much to think about while Rupert was still there, looking a little emotional but fully able to answer my many, many questions.

"Aye," he said. "We had a nice life together, although no bairns - sorry, no children. But we were happy."

"Were?"

"She died, two years ago, when the plague swept through here."

"I'm sorry," I said, wishing life did not have to be full of so much sorrow and heartbreak.

He just nodded, and for a while we sat there, watching as the plants swayed in the wind and a bird picked at the ground in search of worms.

"I'm so glad to have met you," he said eventually, and I smiled at his words.

"Me too," I said. "And at least now I understand, why she felt she had to come here."

He nodded; "She never would be told not to do something."

"That's definitely true." And while the sadness still tore away at every fibre of my being, there was something comforting about being able to discuss her with someone who truly knew her. I had not had that opportunity, since we kept our circle of acquaintances so small, and there was something cathartic about it.

"Was she happy?" he asked, and I was pleased he didn't ask if she had married, for I did not know what to say. I needed to think, I needed to do the calculations, I needed to work out if there were any possibility this man was my father, before I led him to believe he might be.

"I think so," I said. "She worked hard, but we had a home full of laughter and singing and love, so I think she was, in her own way."

"I'm glad," he said, and when he gave an involuntary shiver I realised how long we had been sat on this cold stone bench.

"I'm sorry," I said. "I've kept you far too long, and it is freezing. Perhaps... perhaps we could speak again, before I go back to London?"

He stood and rubbed his hands together to get the blood flowing. "That would be wonderful. Where are you staying?"

I blushed. "Here, actually." He must presume, correctly so, that my mother and I would not have had the means to be connected to anyone like Nicholas, and so I felt an explanation was needed. "I had a fever, when I arrived in the area, and the lord kindly offered for me to stay."

Rupert nodded. "He's a good sort, even if he's been absent the last few years. You're better now, though?"

I nodded. "Just too much time spent in the rain - although I'll be in trouble with the doctor for being out in the cold this long, I'm sure!"

We said our goodbyes, and I watched him walk away through the gardens, feeling a lump rising in my throat.

I needed to think.

*   *   *

My head was reeling as I made my way back

into the house. It seemed I had found my answers, somehow, despite the rocky beginning to my visit here, and although they would not bring my mother back, they at least made some sense of her desperate need to come back here, in spite of her failing health.

I was so sad she had not had the chance to say goodbye to a man it seemed she loved. And now, as I stepped through the stone archway, I was trying desperately to come to terms with the fact that perhaps I was not an orphan after all.

Born on the wrong side of wedlock, for sure - but maybe I wasn't so alone in the world. And that made my heart soar - even if he didn't yet realise he could possibly be my father.

That was a conversation for another day - for now, all I could think of was telling Nicholas how fruitful his lead has been. He would be in the library, I was sure of it, and I practically skipped down the corridor. I couldn't admit to him that my mother had been a maid here - but the fact that she had been in love with a gardener, I felt that he might understand.

I tapped on the door and, hearing him respond, pushed it open. He looked up and smiled immediately, and all thoughts momentarily flew from my mind.

"He says he was in love with my mother!"

I blurted out, without thinking what he might think of me. He stood, and took two steps towards me. "And that he wrote to her, telling her he was ill."

"And so she travelled to see him?"

I nodded. "I think so. It would make sense."

He took my hands, and I focussed on how warm they were and how strong they felt, as his words swirled around us. "I know it won't bring her back," he said, his words once again so amazingly mirroring my thoughts. "But I hope you can find some peace at knowing why she felt she had to travel."

I couldn't tell him I thought Rupert was my father - not before I had confirmed it, and not without thinking through very carefully how it might change his opinion of me.

"Thank you," I whispered, squeezing his hands gently to try to convey how much his words resonated with me. And I couldn't have said who moved first, but his head was dipping towards mine, and I was raising myself up on tiptoes, and finally, finally our lips met. It felt like I had been waiting for that moment since the very first time I had seen him, coming towards me through the mist and rain. Certainly since that moment we had shared in the bedroom, before the fireplace. Even though I had never been kissed before, even though I knew I did not belong in this place or these clothes or this world - I knew I wanted this.

I wanted him.

My arms moved to lock themselves around his neck, and I felt his around my waist, holding me closer, making it quite clear that he wanted this kiss as much as I did.

Our lips moved together and my mind went blank of anything but the feeling of him surrounding me. He pressed me even closer still, if that were possible, and I felt a moan escape my lips. Every part of my body was screaming to be closer to him, just when every part of me should be saying to get the hell away, and fast.

Because this was so, so wrong - but it felt deliciously right, and after the year I'd had, I didn't have the strength in me to deny this pleasure.

Besides, who would care if I was ruined anyway?

"My Lord-"

"Out!" Nicholas shouted as we sprang apart, and I just had a moment to see the shoes of a servant hastily retreating through the doorway, before the veil of embarrassment and shock began to descend over me. I risked a glance at Nicholas, who was breathing as deeply as I, but looked away before we could make eye contact.

To have been discovered in the arms of a man I was not married to was, of course, tantamount to ruin.

But what was even worse was the realisation, as my body returned to its normal temperature away from the heat of his arms, that this was something that would have to come to an end in the very near future. I had been well enough to walk down to see Rupert in the gardens; I had been well enough to be swept into Nicholas's arms.

I was well enough, I supposed, to go home - to go back to my real life, and leave the fairy-tale I had found myself in.

I squeaked an apology and disappeared from the room, needing some time to think without the intensity of his eyes upon me.

CHAPTER TWENTY

Nicholas

She was gone before I could say a word and - if I were truthful - I didn't know what I would have said if I'd had the chance.

I shouldn't have kissed her.

That much was plain; she was an innocent, an unmarried girl, who should not have been in my house, let alone in my arms with my lips upon hers.

And yet...

I had not been the only one enjoying that kiss, that much I knew. And it felt so natural, when she came to me with news that was clearly causing her conflicting emotions. Everything she had said about parents and loss had resonated with me more than she could know, and so to comfort her at this time felt... right.

I sank into my chair and put my head in my hands, the image of her warm body sinking against mine playing over and over in my mind. I had been denying how much I wanted her, I knew that; denying that there had been an attraction between us as soon as we met.

But was there something more?

Had I ever listened to anyone, quite like I did Annelise? Had anyone ever said exactly what I needed to hear?

The answer, of course, was no - but I was not looking for a wife. I had tried that path, and ended up with a bruised ego and a broken heart. I had vowed that marriage and love were no longer important - and that I would not risk my heart again.

And yet here I was, losing my mind over a girl who I knew next to nothing about.

I groaned into my hands, knowing that I had lost whatever argument I was having with myself. I could no longer deny the feelings I had for Annelise Edwards - the question was, what was I to do about them?

CHAPTER TWENTY-ONE
Annelise

I lay in bed, staring at the ceiling, wishing Nicholas would knock on the door and wishing I never had to see him again in equal measure.

I had done something terrible.

Not the kiss, although I knew what society would think of that. No, I had hidden my identity from him, even this afternoon. I had not admitted that I believed the gardener could well be my father. Not admitted that my mother was a maid and that we had lived in tiny buildings that could fit into this one bedchamber my entire life.

And now... and now I knew what it felt like to be in his arms, to feel his lips upon mine, the strength of his body pressed against me - and I felt ashamed for deceiving him.

There could be nothing between us, surely

- not once he knew the truth. A lord and a maid did not wed, that was a story best left to the fairy-tale stories mothers told their children at bedtime. And I could not keep hiding who I was from him - because I was beginning to realise, as difficult as it made things, that I felt something for Nicholas.

Something more than a frisson of passion when he smiled, or when I spent too long staring at the muscles in his arms.

No, I felt something that I knew I would miss when I left here and went back to my life. The feeling of being known, of being understood, that I didn't think I had ever felt before. And I was sure he felt it too - but he didn't have all the facts.

It seemed I had created the perfect situation to have my heart well and truly broken, and I still had to face Nicholas in the morning in the knowledge that we had kissed, and that I had fled the room, and that he would soon want nothing more to do with me.

It was an exquisite kind of pain, and I lay rehashing the evening's events in a strange state of misery and elation, wondering if that kiss, that kiss that took my breath away and made my knees feel like they could not support my weight, would remain with me until my dying day.

CHAPTER TWENTY-TWO
Nicholas

I knew I had consumed far too much wine, but it did not stop me refilling my goblet once more. The fire was dying, but the drink kept me warm, and my thoughts turned once more to the predicament I had got myself in.

I had realised with the third helping of wine that I really knew nothing of Annelise. And that was dangerous in itself; I had thought I had known Bridgitte, and still she had managed to hurt me. A woman I had been acquainted with for mere days - however intense they had been - was surely more likely to hurt me than someone I had known for years.

Swilling the last of the drink round the goblet before knocking it down my throat, I pondered my options. The most sensible, of course, would be to pretend nothing had happened, be polite and wait for her to be on her way.

The other options included kissing her senseless once more, and quite possibility whisking her up the stairs to bed - but that, I knew, was more than my honour could cope with.

And then there was the option in between disinterest and debauchery: marriage.

The thought was there, in my mind, no matter how many times I tried to bat it away. The idea of Annelise in my home, in my bed, at my table, day after day and night and night - it appealed to me in a way I had not thought was possible so soon after Bridgitte, the woman I had presumed would be in the role of my wife.

And yet...

I poured another glass of wine. My head kept trying to dissect every possible outcome. It was going to be a very long night.

◆ ◆ ◆

The after-effects of my over-imbibing the night before were definitely present, and it was late in the morning by the time I had roused myself and splashed some cold water on my face to make me feel somewhat alive.

It had been many months since I had sat and drank so much alone, and it had not managed to obliterate my thoughts like I had hoped it would. All I thought of was her; her lips, her eyes, her words, her body... just her.

I had made up my mind, somewhere in the early hours of the morning when I was still awake, that I would pretend nothing had happened. I would pretend that we had not kissed, that I was not consumed by thoughts of her, that I didn't imagine whisking her into my bedchamber and...

No, I thought to myself, and I shook those ideas from my head. That was not going to help matters. I would pretend things were exactly as they had been, and then she would leave, and I would get the estate sorted, just as I had planned. There had been a plan in place, before she had tumbled into my life and my home; there was no reason to change that.

I dressed without ringing for help, knowing that Harris would only chastise me for drinking too much and not sleeping. Besides, I had spent many years dressing myself, and although, as a lord, I needed to keep up the employment numbers to support society, I could certainly sort my own clothes every now and then.

It was too late for breakfast, but I was sure the staff would have sent some up to Annelise. I also knew I needed to stay away from that bedchamber, lest I give in to some of the many urges that had been in my mind since that kiss.

"Can you invite Miss Edwards to join me for lunch, please?" I asked the maid who I passed on the stairs, and she nodded and scurried away. We would eat together, as we had done several times, and discuss what she had found out.

There would be absolutely no kissing.

I stood in the hallway, momentarily unsure what to do with myself before lunch. I had plenty of work to do, of course, but I knew I would not be able to focus on accounts with my mind in this state. I could go for a ride, but there wasn't really time. Just as I turned for the library, thinking I could at least attempt to continue the volume of Greek myths I had been perusing lately, there was a loud knock at the door.

A tall young man scurried to answer it, and when it opened I felt my heart sink in my chest - despite the fact that the woman at the door was someone I held in very high esteem.

"Aunt Eleanor," I said, a false grin pasted onto my face. The esteem I held her in was part of the problem - that, and the fact that she knew me too well to be taken in by the many lies I was currently telling myself.

"Nicholas!" she exclaimed, removing her cloak and passing it to the young servant. She took two steps towards me, looked me up and down, and then furrowed her brow. "You've been drinking too much."

I sighed. "Nice to see you too, Aunt."

She pulled me into a hug that was warm and inviting, despite her words, before pulling back to look into my face more closely.

"It's always nice to see you, although I admit I thought it would be harder to track you down than finding you on the other side of your front door!"

I smiled at that; she was right, of course. Normally she would not have been quite so lucky as to find me within moments of her arrival. There had been several times she had visited to find me away, or at court, or even just out riding.

"Well, you're in luck today. Will you stay for lunch?"

"And dinner too, if it's offered!" she said with a grin that lit up her face and made her look ten years younger. She was my mother's sister, and the resemblance between the two was clear, even to me. Even though it had been so long since I had looked upon my mother's face...

"Of course, you know you're always welcome." I threaded her arm through mine and escorted her through to the dining room. "What brings you to the area?"

"I'm visiting my son, up North, but you know how long it takes to get there. I have to break the journey up, and I thought who better to drop in on unannounced than my favourite nephew!"

I laughed. "Only nephew, you mean. Will you stay the night?"

"If you're sure you have the room," she said, sarcasm flooding her voice.

"Oh, I think we'll manage."

For a few moments, for the first time in days, Annelise had not been at the forefront of my mind. But when we entered the dining hall, and I saw her sat at the table in a pink dress that made her look so delicate, so beautiful, all my thoughts returned and left me as breathless as if I had been punched in the gut.

"Oh, I did not realise you had company, Nicholas," Eleanor said with a raised eyebrow, and years of practice allowed me to hear so much behind her words. Questions, comments, judgments - all of which I was sure to hear out loud, later.

Annelise looked a little like a frightened deer, and I spoke quickly to avoid her bolting. "Your arrival surprised me, Aunt, I didn't think to mention it straight away. This is Annelise Edwards. Annelise, this is my Aunt, Eleanor Hambury."

Annelise stood, looking awkward. "It's a pleasure to meet you," she said.

"And you, my dear - although I didn't quite catch your connection to my Nicholas."

Nicholas cringed at the tone, as he pulled out a chair for Eleanor opposite the one Annelise was using. He motioned for wine to be poured, and took his seat at the head of the table.

"Annelise was visiting Marvale to find out about her mother, who has sadly passed away," he said, hoping his tone would warn his aunt of further questioning. "She fell very ill, and has been staying here while she recovers."

Her eyes widened sharply at that, but she did not say what was going through her mind. "Indeed," was all that passed her lips, before she sipped her wine and regarded Annelise across the table.

"How are you feeling today?" I asked her, knowing that this situation forced me to act as though nothing had happened. Perhaps it was for the best.

"B-better, thank you, my lord," she said, and I inwardly sighed at the loss of 'Nicholas'. But again, perhaps it was for the better... I could now only think of my name as a sigh on her lips, those lips I had kissed so thoroughly...

"And how is Marvale doing?" my aunt asked, and I forced my attention back to her as the food was brought to the table.

CHAPTER TWENTY-THREE
Annelise

Being in the presence of a relative of his, someone dressed so finely and with such flawless speech, burst whatever bubble I had been living in.

I did not belong here.

Of course I had known that all along, but in the seven days I had been in this house, wearing borrowed dresses and sleeping in a bed made for someone far higher in society than I, it had been easy to forget that I was an impostor here.

But when Nicholas's aunt had stepped into the room, I remembered very swiftly. And what was worse, it felt as though she knew it too. Every look, every comment, every discussion that was about people I would never have heard of, let alone met - it all made in perfectly clear that I did not belong.

I shrank into the chair, wishing I could disappear, and even contemplated pretending to faint, just to escape this dinner. But then Nicholas might worry, or carry me, and the thought of his hands on my body made me lose my train of thought.

We were clearly pretending that kiss in the library hadn't happened. As though I had not spent every moment of the night reliving it.

"Annelise?"

I blinked, realising both pairs of eyes were on me. Clearly I had missed whatever part of the conversation was related to me, and my cheeks flushed in embarrassment.

"I'm sorry?"

"I was just asking what your plans are," Eleanor said, with a smile I did not quite trust. "Now that you have recovered from your illness."

I swallowed, knowing it was a question I had been avoiding. "I shall be heading home," I said, hoping that she would not delve too deeply into where exactly home was. I was too flustered to lie well, I knew that. "I have found out about my mother's connections, and so my business is complete."

I did not meet Nicholas's eye. Would he be

disappointed? Or, more likely, would he be relieved that this burden that had appeared on his doorstep would be moving on?

Even if he did seem to enjoy kissing me, I could readily believe it was the latter.

"If you'll excuse me," I said, as soon as the last dish was cleared away. "I am still feeling rather tired. I think I will lie down for a while."

Nicholas stood, but I did not give him the opportunity to say anything, if he had indeed been planning to. I disappeared out of the doorway and up the stairs as quickly as I could in the heavy dress, not wanting to hear the discussion of me that would inevitably follow such a meal.

Once in my room, I paced the floor, too worked up to actually lie down on the bed. I would have to leave, within the next day or two, now that I had said it. And besides, there was nothing keeping me here now. I had my answers.

The previous night had certainly been a sleepless one, and not only because of the fiery kiss I had shared with Nicholas. No, I had also rehashed everything Rupert had said to me, and the more I thought on it, the more I believed he truly could be my father. After all, I knew that Mother had left Marvale in the months before I was born. From what I had known of her, she had never been obviously interested in any men of our acquaintance

- and so I found it hard to believe that there were many candidates for who my father was. I had never understood why she wouldn't tell me more, but I also had never pushed harder when it obviously grieved her.

I wished I had now.

What I could not understand, if my theory was correct, was why she'd left. If she'd been in love with Rupert, if she'd... done whatever was necessary to produce a child - and I was still a little hazy on the finer points of that, other than knowing it was not acceptable outside of marriage - and if she'd known Rupert was willing to break his betrothal...

Why had she left?

Why had she not married the man I presumed she had loved?

Something didn't seem to add up. Perhaps, I thought as I paced the length of the room once more, Rupert had not told me the whole truth. Or perhaps my mother had reasons that would never be uncovered.

I finally threw myself on the bed, giving in to a few racking sobs of frustration at the fact that I would never have the chance to ask her any of this.

CHAPTER TWENTY-FOUR
Nicholas

As soon as she left the room, I prepared myself for my aunt's attack, hoping she at least had the sense to wait for Annelise to be far away enough to not overhear.

I loved my aunt, I always had - but she certainly didn't pull her punches.

"Nicholas."

She surveyed me over her hands, which were folded neatly under her chin.

"Yes?" I met her gaze, refusing to apologise when I had done nothing wrong.

"This girl-"

"Annelise." I did not know why I was correcting her. I knew I should not; knew she should be 'Miss Edwards' and nothing more, but I could not think of her as anything other than *Annelise*.

"Miss Edwards," Eleanor said, and I heard the reproach in her voice. "Has stayed in this house for seven nights. Is that correct?"

"Tonight will be the seventh," I countered.

"So the two of you," she said, lips pursed, "An unmarried man and an unmarried woman, have been under the same roof for the last six nights, without a chaperone?"

"Ah-" She had me there. And I couldn't pretend to be oblivious, because of course the thought had crossed my mind too. "Yes," I finally said, my head hanging a little. "But nothing has-"

I didn't get to finish the lie. "I don't care what has or hasn't happened, Nicholas! You are a lord, for goodness sake. It is totally improper. You know nothing of her, for one, and you've already damaged your reputation enough with the other one jilting you at the altar."

I didn't correct her on the name this time. *The other one* did not deserve my intervention. Still, I cringed at the reminder of my failings.

"And beyond that, the girl's reputation is ruined. Can't you see that? She will never be able to marry if word of this gets out - and with the number of staff you have here, you can be sure word *will* get out."

My head dropped lower. She was right, of course she was. And it wasn't just rumours that we had been in the house together; my staff had seen me carry her in, carry her up the stairs, sit beside her bed. Not to mention the poor soul who had been unfortunate enough to walk in on our embrace last night.

I had ruined her. Without even acting on my baser instincts, I had still managed to ruin her reputation. I doubted she had thought about it, but she was an innocent, with no parents in the world to look out for her. I knew better, and yet I had taken advantage of her without even meaning to.

"You're right," I said, softly, reaching for my wine and draining it in one gulp.

She huffed. "Of course I am." Then, clearly realising the impact her words had on me, she reached out to lay a hand on my forearm.

"Nicholas, dear. You know how fond I am of you. And I know the last few months have not been easy for you."

I nodded, not sure what more to say. My head had moved away from this conversation, anyway, to what I could do to rectify the situation.

"I trust you will deal with this?" she said, and I nodded.

I did not know what exactly she had in mind, but I knew what I must do.

◆ ◆ ◆

Thankfully, her journey - combined with lecturing me, I was sure - had tired my aunt out, and as much as she hated to show her age, she stifled a yawn and eventually asked to be shown to her room for a rest before dinner.

I knew I should really be spending that time working, since the rest of the day had been so wasted, but I also knew that I would not be going near the accounts today. Butterflies swarmed in my stomach, and I regretted eating so heavily. What I needed to do and what I wanted to do were somehow aligned, and yet my nerves overtook my thoughts in a way I was not used to.

If I delayed, I knew I would talk myself out of this action, and so as soon as the bedroom door closed on my aunt I strode purposefully to the other end of the house, and rapped on Annelise's door.

She opened it in a heartbeat, fully dressed with red rings around her eyes that told me she had been crying. I hated being the cause of any more pain for this beautiful woman - but when she offered me a shy smile, I could not help but return it.

She stepped aside to let me in, and I shut the door behind us, propriety be damned. The air seemed to fizzle around us, and before she could say anything, I started to speak.

"Annelise," I said, focusing on her face as if I were trying to commit it to memory. "I have been remiss. This past week, we have lived together under one roof without anyone to chaperone, and I am ashamed to say I have ruined your reputation." I did not speak of the kiss the previous night, although the blush on her cheeks suggested that we both remembered it very well indeed.

"I can only apologise, and ask you if you would do me the honour of taking my hand in marriage - of becoming my wife."

CHAPTER TWENTY-FIVE
Annelise

I laughed. I didn't mean to, but the whole situation was just so ridiculous, I could not help myself. This Lord, this beautiful Greek God of a man, was worried about my reputation. Was asking me to marry him! I could not have dreamed such a scenario, and yet here it was, in this ornate bedroom - a scene from a story, not real life.

His face screwed up at my ill-timed laughter. "Annelise, do you understand? I am asking you to marry me."

"No!" It burst from my lips without my permission, but I saw the hurt on his face before he replaced it with a dispassionate mask.

"Can I ask why?" he asked, and I wondered which of the many reasons to tell him.

"Can we sit, Nicholas?" I asked softly, and he

nodded, collapsing into a chair by the fire while I perched on the edge of the bed.

"I haven't been honest with you," I said, taking a deep breath before forcing the words out. "And I'm sorry. I'm - I'm the daughter of a maid. The bastard daughter of a maid, I think, and a gardener, although I'm not completely sure about that yet." When he didn't speak I continued, offering him every explanation to why I was so rudely rejecting his offer of marriage.

"My mother was a maid here, before I was born. And she spent her life taking in washing - as have I. This last week..." I laughed again, wondering at my ability to somehow find humour in one of the most painful moments of my life. "This last week has been like a fairy tale. But I don't belong here. And as gallant as your offer is..." I gave a sad smile, my eyes meeting his for just a moment. "No-one cares about my reputation. No-one will care that I'm ruined. I'm not important enough for anyone to even know that I was in this house with you, without supervision." No-one would know that we had kissed, either - but I knew I would think of it as often as I could.

I looked to the floor, embarrassment over my deception flooding my chest. "I'm sorry, that I misled you. You owe me nothing - in fact, you've been nothing but generous."

Silence hovered around us for a few moments that stretched on and on.

And then he broke the moment with a curt "Very well."

And then he was gone.

And my heart shattered into the million pieces I had always known it would end up in.

CHAPTER TWENTY-SIX

Nicholas

I paced the library, wishing the house were empty of guests and I could get as drunk as I needed to. Yet again, a woman had thrown me aside - without a thought for my emotions. Once again I had put my heart on the line, and been rewarded with it being thrown back in my face.

Somehow, this was worse than with Bridgitte. I couldn't explain how, considering I had known her years, and Annelise mere days - but I was sure this pain was greater.

I knocked back a strong drink, and paused to look out of the window. The clouds rolled in with, I imagined, yet another storm, and darkness was falling around us. For miles I could see animals, houses, crops - all relying on Marvale to make sure they would continue to be profitable. It was a burden I had not thought of, when I was a young lad living here, or when I was gallivanting at court - but it weighed heavily on my mind now.

I wished it was my only concern.

I didn't care that she was the daughter of a maid, I realised as I poured another drink. I had suspected she was not from my class, and the information I had learnt from the tenant farmer's mother had all but confirmed that. I could understand, even, why she had kept it from me - but when I had offered her marriage, to share my name, my home, my life - she had laughed.

She had said no.

And that hurt more than I would ever let anyone know.

I wished I never had to set eyes on a woman again - but unfortunately there were two staying in my home, and I knew I could not avoid them forever.

CHAPTER TWENTY-SEVEN
Annelise

I couldn't go down for dinner, not when I had refused his proposal. A nervous laugh bubbled up every time I thought of him, stood in front of me, offering me *marriage*.

Could I imagine being married to him?

For a second, just a second, I let my mind imagine being Nicholas's wife. Living in this house, eating the rich food that seemed to be served for every meal, kissing him whenever I liked... It made my cheeks flush red, and that was without thoughts of being his *wife* in truth, sharing his bed, having children with him.

But I only let myself imagine for a moment because, of course, it was ridiculous. He knew now, that I was nothing - and I was sure he would expect me to leave as soon as was possible.

I needed to speak with Rupert one more

time, needed to discuss the fact that I thought he could be my father, before leaving this area forever. He could think on it, then, and perhaps we could write. It made me feel a little better to at least know that I might have someone in this world who I was connected to. It felt mighty lonely, thinking I had no-one left.

And then I would go.

A day or two, hopefully, depending on the weather, and I could be gone from this house. Gone from Nicholas. Gone from the strangest week of my life.

CHAPTER TWENTY-EIGHT
Nicholas

I refrained from having a third drink, and made my way down to dinner, wondering what I would be facing. When I entered the great hall, it was empty, and I breathed a brief sigh of relief.

It was short-lived, however; Aunt Eleanor strode through the door moments later, and I stood as she sat down.

"Did you manage to rest, Aunt?" I asked, and she nodded.

"I feel ten years younger," she said with a smile. "You do have the most comfortable beds at Marvale. I always said my brother-in-law had great taste."

I smiled, waiting for the inevitable questioning to begin, whilst keeping one eye on the door. I did not think Annelise would show, and when the first course was served and she still had not appeared, I realised my hunch was correct.

"Can you ask Cook to send some food to Miss Edwards, please," I asked the serving girl, and she nodded and disappeared from the table.

"Is Miss Edwards still unwell?" Eleanor asked, clearly fishing for information.

"I wouldn't know," I said. I knew none of this was Eleanor's fault, knew that she'd certainly had a valid point about Annelise staying here alone - and yet I could not help but feel frustrated that she had popped this bubble we had been living in, had forced me to propose; and then to be rejected.

"Ah." She said. She lifted the bread to her lips, and I thought she wanted to say something, but she seemed to think better of it.

We ate mainly in silence, until Eleanor reached across from the side of the table and squeezed my arm.

"I just want you to be happy, Nicholas," she said. "You do know that, don't you?"

I nodded, but there was nothing I could say. I wasn't happy, and I didn't know how to be.

I was angry; I was frustrated; I was sad.

And there was nothing I could do about that.

CHAPTER TWENTY-NINE
Annelise

I got up with the sun and sneaked from the house before anyone was awake. I had tried to eat the dinner that was sent up the night before, but I couldn't stomach most of it, and I felt the same after a sleepless night.

Even in the early morning light, the clouds looked ominous, and I hoped I would be able to leave the next day. I would need most of a day to travel, and so I knew I wouldn't be able to safely leave today - but I definitely needed to speak with Rupert first.

I just hoped he was awake this early.

As I rounded the corner, I saw him on his knees, pulling something from the ground. I imagined in the summer this place would be full of flowers, bees and butterflies - but for now it was mainly green, and I watched for a moment as Rupert tended to it, before alerting him to my presence.

He turned, and a smile appeared on his face when he saw me stood there. "Oh! Annelise, I am pleased to see you again."

"And I you," I said, as he slowly stood, clearly struggling a little to get off the ground. "I hope I'm not stopping you working."

He dusted off his hands. "I was just making the most of a bit of dry weather," he said. "But I've got time to talk, if you'd like."

I nodded. "I remembered a cloak this time!"

He laughed; "That's good. Shall we walk?"

For a few moments we walked down the lush green pathway, and Rupert pointed out some of the plants that grew there. I had been a London girl for most of my life, and so I had little knowledge of flowers and herbs, but it was fascinating to hear how much he cared about them.

And then we reached the lake, that very same lake I had stared into in the middle of a raging storm. It looked different now, a calm mirror in the middle of wild greenery, but I gave a little shiver as I thought of that day, of everything that had begun in that moment.

"I have something I need to tell you," I said,

pausing by the lake and fiddling with my fingers. There was no easy way to say these words, and it was an awkward conversation to be having - but I knew I could not leave Marvale without letting my thoughts be known.

"I am twenty years old," I said with a deep breath to spur me on. "And I wondered, when we spoke the other day..." My eyes met his for a second, and I forced myself to finish the sentence. "I wondered if there was any chance you could be my father."

"Your father?"

I nodded, and waited for him to say something. He seemed to freeze, for a moment, and then his face softened.

"I... yes. It would be possible. But I don't understand..."

"Shall we sit?" I asked, and he nodded and followed me to another stone bench. This news was bound to shock, and the last thing I wanted was him collapsing in front of me in the grounds of Marvale.

"I have never been told much about my father," I said, filling the silence with nervous chatter. "My mother said she loved him, and could not be with him. That... that was all I knew. And I'd never met anyone who said he had been in love with her - before you..."

He looked at me, tears in his eyes, and I felt my grip on my emotions begin to wobble. It had all been so much to take in, this week - learning about Rupert, realising who he could be, let alone the swirl of emotions that took over my body and mind whenever I thought of Nicholas.

"It is possible," he said. "We... we loved each other. But surely she would have said something? If I had known... Annelise, you have to believe me, if this is true I had no idea of your existence. I never would have left Elise to raise a child alone."

"I know that," I said, and somehow I did, even though I barely knew this man. "I don't know why she wouldn't say anything - she was a stubborn woman, a proud woman, as I'm sure you knew. But this... I don't really understand. And I guess we'll never know."

He nodded and we both looked out at the beautiful gardens for a moment, letting the situation we were in wash over us.

"We'll never know," he said. "Whether you are my... my daughter, or why she left. But... I would be honoured to have you as my daughter, if you were looking for a father."

Tears fell from my eyes and I didn't even bother to try to stop them. I nodded, though, and he reached over and squeezed my hand. The tears fell down my cheeks, dropping on my hands, and it took me a few moments to realise it had started to rain - that the droplets on my skin were not just from my tears. Without speaking, we stood and dashed to a stone archway for cover, and I took the opportunity to swipe the sleeve of my cloak across my eyes.

"I'm sorry," I said, looking at this man who was the only person in the world I had a link to. "It's just... I thought I was completely alone."

"Me too, Lass. Me too." And then his arms were around me, and I returned the hug with a warm heart and a few more tears threatening to fall.

"You're returning to London, soon?" he asked.

I nodded. "Tomorrow, probably. But I could write..."

"Aye. And I could visit London, I reckon, if I got permission from the lord."

I put Nicholas from my mind and nodded at the suggestion.

I did not understand my mother's motives for leaving, and I did not know if this man was in truth my father. But he was happy to say he was, and that was absolutely good enough for me.

CHAPTER THIRTY
Nicholas

I scowled at the rain falling from the sky, as I nursed a headache and regretted, once again, drinking far too much. After our quiet dinner, Aunt Eleanor had gone to bed and I had drunk, and drunk, and drunk...

And now I could not go for a ride, could not leave the house, because the infernal rain had started again. I could not go and talk to Annelise, because she had said no to my proposal of marriage, and there was nothing to say to my aunt.

I knew, however, I needed to say goodbye to my aunt, and so once I was semi-decent, I headed out of the door and down the stairs - only to run into Annelise, coming through the front door. She was wearing a cloak, but the rain clearly dripped from her skin, and I opened my mouth in wonder that she could be so stupid for a second time.

"Do you have a death wish?" I asked her, my voice harsher than I intended, and her mouth formed a circle of shock. I instantly regretted my words, but there was no way to take them back.

"It wasn't raining, when I went outside," she said timidly.

"I've heard that before," I said with a huff, and then stomped towards the dining room, knowing that being in her presence would only lead to me saying something even ruder.

I needed to be alone today - and I needed to not drink to excess tonight. Tomorrow, surely, would be a better day.

CHAPTER THIRTY-ONE
Annelise

For a few moments I stood in the hallway, dripping on his expensive wooden floors, shocked at the way he had spoken to me. Yes, he knew I was the daughter of a maid, and I supposed I should be grateful he had not kicked me out - but was there any need to speak to me in such an awful way?

I tried not to dwell on it as I trudged upstairs and removed the layers of wet clothing. I had not intended to get caught in the rain, but my talk with Rupert had been decidedly more important than a few dark clouds, and in truth I had only got wet as I ran back to the house - despite how drenched I looked.

I struggled to unlace the dress by myself, and once it was off there was the even more challenging job of re-dressing myself in one of the borrowed dresses that had been left in the room for me to use. I might not have bothered, but I knew I needed to speak to Nicholas, to tell him I was leaving - and I needed to be properly attired for that.

At a knock on the door I froze, but when I called out and heard Edith's response, I breathed a sigh of relief.

"What good timing!" I said, a smile on my face as she rushed over to help me. "I cannot get this thing on by myself, no matter how hard I try. And I got caught in that dreadful rain shower!"

She clicked her tongue at me. "You want to stay out of the wet, m'lady!" she said.

"I've told you, it's Annelise." I had not told Edith of my humble background, for fear of embarrassing Nicholas if the truth got out, but I certainly did not want a false title being bestowed upon me.

She smiled, and said nothing, and when she next spoke the dress was securely in place.

"There you are. No more walks in the rain! Lord Gifford said you'd been out in it again."

I paused at that; had he sent Edith up, after seeing the state of me? If so, it seemed a surprisingly thoughtful act, especially after the way he had spoken to me.

Edith lit the fire, and left me alone with my

thoughts - which, these days, seemed a rather tempestuous place to be.

◆ ◆ ◆

I presumed he would be in the library, since the weather did not really allow for outside activities, and so I headed towards it, trying to talk myself into seeming confident. I needed to tell him this, and it needed to be today - so I might as well get it over and done with.

Reaching the door, I took one more deep breath and raised my hand to knock - before hearing voices coming down the stairs. I darted into the small sitting room, which was mercifully empty, listening through the open door to Nicholas and his aunt.

"Are you sure you should be travelling, in this?" Nicholas asked, although his tone was a lot more polite than when he had been questioning me about being out in the rain.

"Oh, Nicholas," she said with a sigh. "It's a passing shower, that's all. Your cousin is expecting me, and I should not impose on your hospitality any longer."

"Aunt Eleanor..." he said, and I wished I could see his face as he spoke. There was hurt in his voice, I was sure, although I did not quite understand where it came from. "You know you can stay as long as you like. You're family."

"Thank you, dear boy," she said, and through the gap in the door I saw her raise her hand and place it on his cheek, just for a moment. "You deserve happiness, Nicholas. Find someone who's deserving of your name, and your heart."

My heart dropped to my stomach. *Deserving*. Rich, and titled then, I presumed. Not the daughter of a maid... Not someone who had hidden her identity.

I disappeared back into the shadows in case one of them looked my way, and left them to their goodbyes, unwatched. Instead I stood and looked as the rain ran down the windowpanes, and in the distance filled the lake. Had any February ever been so wet? I felt as though I had seen enough rain to last my entire lifetime - and yet still it fell.

I could not say how long I waited there, but when silence had fallen in the corridor, I peeked round the door and - upon reassuring myself no-one was around - made my way back to the library.

I steeled myself to look into his dark, brooding eyes once more, as I raised my fist and knocked.

CHAPTER THIRTY-TWO

Nicholas

"Come in," I said, wondering what was needed of me now. I had felt lonely for so long, but now that I needed to be alone with my thoughts, it seemed I could never get a moment's peace.

The door swung open, and she walked in with her head held high. For a moment no thoughts existed in my mind, save for memories of kissing her in this very library. Her lips looked a tempting red, perhaps from her reckless behaviour in the rain, yet she wore a fresh dress that showed no sign of the damp weather.

It took me a while to realise I was staring without speaking, and I coughed to cover the slip. "Good afternoon," I said, as politely as I could, aware that I needed to exercise exceptional self-control if I were to avoid making a fool of myself once more.

"Good afternoon," she said, in a voice higher than normal, and I wondered if I made her nervous. I tried to keep my breath even as I imagined closing the gap between us, shoving this desk out of the way and taking her in my arms like-

No.

This had to stop. She needed to leave my home before I tried to seduce her, before I ruined her reputation any further - or lost my mind enough to offer marriage once more.

When I didn't speak, she carried on. Her words almost sounded rehearsed, and I wondered how long she had planned to say them.

"I wanted to thank you," she said, attempting a smile that did not stay in place. "For your generous hospitality, especially when I was ill. I know it has been a burden, and I truly appreciate everything you have done."

"It was no bother," I said, a little gruffly, making eye contact only briefly. I couldn't bear to think back to that night where I had slept on the floor of her room, holding her hand, willing her to get better. I could not think of being so intimate with a woman I would never see again.

My words hurt her, I was fairly sure, and I gripped the table to stop myself taking them back. It was better this way.

"Well," she said eventually. "I am grateful, all the same. And I know I have overstayed my welcome, so I wanted you to know I plan to leave tomorrow. I believe I can catch the coach back to the city."

I blinked back my disgust at the thought of her on the coach, crammed in with all manner of miscreants and drunkards. But she was not my responsibility, and I supposed that was how she had got here in the first place; thinking on it, I had never even asked.

"Very well," I said, and her eyes widened a little at the lack of feeling in my tone. Even I was shocked, but my hand was gripping the desk so hard my knuckles were practically white, and I could not focus on my tone as well.

With a polite nod, she turned on her heels and closed the door, and I finally let go of the solid wood before me. Blood rushed back into my fingers as I took several harsh breaths, telling myself in no uncertain terms that I could not ask her to stay.

I wanted her gone; I wanted to be alone with my thoughts.

More than that, I could not ask her to stay because she was not mine. I had asked her that already - and she had said no.

CHAPTER THIRTY-THREE
Annelise

I refused to let the tears fall from my eyes as I made my way back to the bedroom. It felt like a prison, despite how luxurious it was, because I had known time with Nicholas both in it and outside it - and now I must confine myself to it alone.

It felt like I was losing something, even though I had never had it to begin with, and my mind would not allow me to leave those thoughts behind. It was a long time until dinner, when I supposed I might leave my room to dine with Nicholas, and so on a whim I turned on my heel and headed to the kitchens. It was a hive of activity and so, for a moment, I just watched. I could imagine my mother down here. She had always been a hard worker, but she also loved to laugh and joke and sing, and this seemed liked a happy household to be in - unless you were the lord, of course.

Edith turned, and gasped as she saw me in the doorway.

"M'lady!" she said, rubbing floury hands on her apron and taking two steps towards me. "I didn't see you there, I'm sorry."

"I've told you, it's Annelise," I said, wishing I could tell her everything, to talk to her about living here and working here and how my mother would have found it. I wanted anything that would get me closer to my mother, now she had gone - but even with the harsh way Nicholas had spoken to me, I did not want to embarrass him.

He had probably saved my life, out in that storm. Who knew how ill I would have been if I had stayed out longer - or what would have happened to me if I had collapsed somewhere public, on my way home?

Edith laughed nervously. "Can I get you anything?"

"I was wondering if you knew where my dress was? The one I arrived in."

"It's been laundered, I think," she said. "I can get it for you now, if you like?"

"Please," I said. "I'll need it for tomorrow."

Her eyes widened. "Are you leaving?"

I chuckled. "I am. It's long overdue - but I am fully recovered, and must go home."

"Oh." She was silent for a moment, but looked as though words were fighting to escape her lips - but then she turned to find the dress.

"Edith?" I said, and she turned to face me, chewing her bottom lip. "Was there something else you wanted to say?"

"It's not my place..." she said.

"You can say anything you like to me," I said. "I promise."

She paused, then grabbed my arm and dragged me into the corridor, away from the nosy ears of other staff, I presumed. "I've never seen Lord Gifford look at anyone the way he does you. When he sat with you all night, when you had that fever - he slept on the floor! He has never done that before."

I nodded, pondering her words. She obviously felt her meaning was obvious, but I wasn't quite sure what she was suggesting.

"So..."

"So... well, I suppose I thought there might be something between you."

I laughed; I couldn't help it. It was preposterous - just as preposterous as when Nicholas had proposed marriage.

"Lord Gifford is very pleased I'm leaving," I told her, hoping to silence any rumours that might be going around. "He simply took care of me when I became ill in his home."

She nodded, and ducked her head. "Right you are, Miss. I'll just get your dress." And then she was gone, and I did not call her back. What could I say? I knew her words weren't totally fictitious - there had been *something* between us, if that kiss were anything to go by. But I also knew he had only offered his hand out of chivalry, and that I did not belong in this world.

It was not fair to tie him to me forever because of an act of kindness - even if my daydreams about the situation made it very tempting indeed.

CHAPTER THIRTY-FOUR
Nicholas

I sat alone, once more, staring down the long table and wishing it were not quite so empty. I tried not to think of the specifics of who I would like to be sat there, but an image of a wife and several children sat along the mahogany surface made me feel a warmth that I did not really understand. I remembered sitting further down the table, opposite my sister, with Father at the head and Mother at his side, enjoying the meal and the conversation. I had later realised it was not always this way, for rich families; often the children dined with the nanny, and were not seen at the table. But that had never been the case in our household, and I was thankful for it.

Except now, it meant I knew what this room was missing. Laughter, arguments, teasing, jokes - it had seen it all, many, many nights over. And now it was treated to silence.

My wine was topped up, and just as my stomach growled in anticipation of the food that was soon to come, the door opened, and she walked through it.

As if I had not snapped at her, or dismissed her news of leaving.

A vision in red today, she held her head high as she walked to the seat I had already begun to think of as hers, and sat as I belatedly stood.

"Good evening," she said, avoiding my eye.

"Good evening."

My mind was blank. After everything, she still wanted to have dinner with me? She could have avoided me, could have stayed in her room and eaten the meal and left in the morning - but she was here.

With me.

"Did you find answers to all your questions?" I found myself asking as food was placed in front of us. Hunger was no longer on my mind, now she was here before me, but I ate just to have something to do with my hands.

She smiled, and nodded. "I did, thank you."

"I love a mystery," I repeated, knowing I had already told her that. "Would you fill me in?"

CHAPTER THIRTY-FIVE
Annelise

I was so confused by his change in attitude, for a moment I just stared at him, before realising how rude that was. I had come to dinner because I could not face sitting in that room alone again, especially when I knew this was the last night I could sit and dine with him; probably the last night I would dine with anyone for a long time.

But after his attitude this morning, I had not expected him to actually want to talk with me - not like he had before.

I took a bite of bread, giving myself a moment before I had to respond to him. There were no secrets anymore; he knew the worst, and I was leaving in the morning. I could be totally honest - and that was a thrilling thought.

"I believe," I said, when I had finally finished

my mouthful. "That Mr Stockwall might be my father." I thought I might have told him as much when I had told him why I could not marry him, but I wasn't sure whether he had connected the dots.

"Ah," he said with a smile. "Hence why she wanted to come back when he said he was ill."

I nodded; he clearly had been listening.

"They were in love, I think, when she..." I paused, and bit my lip, but pushed on. "When she worked here. And I don't really understand why she left. But it seems likely that he is my father - and..."

When I didn't continue, he prompted me. "And?"

"I know, what everyone would think, if they knew my parents weren't married. I know it was... wrong." I blushed, knowing I was speaking of things I didn't truly understand, but once again feeling the urge to tell him everything I was feeling. For so long I had kept everything to myself; to have the opportunity to share was a joy, even if it were only short-lived. "But knowing that there might be somebody out there who has a connection with me..." I shrugged, and reached out for the wine that had been placed in front of me. "It makes everything feel a little bit better."

He nodded, and for a while we ate in silence.

I wondered if I had shocked him, with the fact that I was born on the wrong side of marriage - or that it didn't bother me.

"I feel the same," he said, when he had finished his meal and leant back a little in his chair. "About my aunt. Even though she can be a little... overbearing." He smiled a little, and I couldn't help but return it. I had other words I might use to describe his aunt in my head, but I certainly wasn't about to share. "But she's family. She's my connection to my mother, and she cares about me - and I certainly can't say that about many people."

He laughed at that, but I felt my heart constricting in my chest. *I care.* I wanted so badly to tell him, wanted to reach out and take his hand and tell him that in the short time I had known him I had begun to care deeply about his happiness.

But of course I could not, and so I simply nodded, and waited for him to continue the conversation.

"So," he said, when all the food was gone and I was feeling full and a little drowsy. "You must leave tomorrow?"

I nodded; it was how it had to be. This could not last, we both knew it. Even if for tonight there was some truce, some unspoken arrangement to pretend as though he had not asked me to marry him, and I had not turned him down.

"How about another game of chess, then?" he asked, and although I knew I should refuse, I also knew there was no possibility of that happening.

"That would be lovely."

CHAPTER THIRTY-SIX

Nicholas

I was clinging on to something that wasn't mine to keep; a feeling that belonged to another man, another home. I followed her to the chess board, watching as the light of my candle danced on the bare skin at her neck. It would be so easy to dip my head, to press my lips to that skin...

That was why spending time with her was a mistake - but one I could not seem to stop making. She would be leaving tomorrow, and I wanted to soak up the time I had left with her. When would I dine again with someone who understood me like she did? When would I play chess with a woman who was focussed on the game, on our conversation, and not just what she was out to gain?

We sat and I set the board up, giving her the white pieces once more. "You can borrow my coach, if you wish," I said, wondering if this was another offer she would refuse. "To take you back to London."

She gasped, but did not immediately refuse. "How would you get it back?"

"I could send someone with you," I said. "I'd... I'd feel better, knowing you had been returned safely. Anyone might be on a public coach."

She nodded, and tipped her head slightly. "I think I probably count as 'anyone'."

"Not to me," I said, without really thinking. Her cheeks blushed at the admission, and I imagined mine did too.

"That would be very generous, my lord," she said.

"Nicholas." If we only had these precious hours, I did not want her calling me 'my lord'. I wanted to be Nicholas, and her to be Annelise, as we had been from the beginning.

"Thank you, Nicholas." Her voice was soft but genuine, and she flashed me a brilliant smile before making the first move on the board.

"What is your home like?" I asked, wishing I could picture where she would be when she no longer occupied the Blue Room.

She blushed again, and I moved my piece, not really caring whether I won or lost.

"Small," she said. "Two rooms - but we've made it comfortable. Mother and I..." She paused and moved another piece, but I was sure she was trying to take control of her emotions.

"We always did well enough, there. It's surrounded by people and businesses, never a moment's peace. You can walk two minutes and see the River Thames, though!"

"I can't imagine living somewhere so busy!" I said, not focussing on her comments about the size. I could picture it now, and my mind could not help thinking that she had chosen to go back to such a small dwelling over being the mistress of this house - over being my wife.

"You've lived at court!" she said with a laugh, remembering to continue the game - something I was already forgetting existed. "I'm sure you know what busy is like."

"Well," I said, with a nod. "I suppose so. But here, there is so much space, so much land - I guess when I think of home, here is where I imagine. The quiet, the animals, the distance between me and all my neighbours."

"It sounds a little lonely," she said, and of course she was right.

My eyes met hers in the glittering light from the fireplace. "It isn't when this house is full of family. Full of love."

She nodded, and the look we shared became so intense I knew I should break away - but I couldn't.

Suddenly, I saw what I had been missing. Yes, she had rejected me - but not like Bridgitte had. She had turned down my money, my name, and yes, my heart - because she believed it was the right thing to do. Even if it meant going back to a life of hard work, plain food and a small home. Even if it meant being alone.

But I didn't want to be alone.

And I could not imagine myself with anyone but her.

CHAPTER THIRTY-SEVEN
Annelise

"It's your turn, Nicholas," I said, when the tension in the room felt like it might explode around us. His words touched my heart, and I found myself thinking back to a day or so previously, when I had watched him in the courtyard from my bedroom window. He was playing with a child, of perhaps five or six. The boy was scruffily dressed, and Nicholas of course had looked immaculate. And yet, when the boy showed him his wooden ball and cup, Nicholas had demonstrated to him how to use it, again and again, until the little boy was laughing and clapping with glee.

And when the boy had eventually managed to copy Nicholas, he had swooped him off the floor and flown him across the sky like a bird, with not a care in the world for who might be watching or how much dust was covering his clothes.

I had asked Edith, later, whom such a boy might belong to, and she had explained that the cook had a son who lived with her in the village, and often came up to help in the gardens.

And now, as our eyes met and the atmosphere crackled around us, and he spoke of love and family, all I could see was him playing in the dust with that little boy.

Had I made a terrible mistake, when I had said no to his proposal?

The moment flickered away as he moved a piece, and I drew a deep breath before taking my turn.

He stared at the board in silence, and I wondered what was on his mind, and whether it mirrored my own very jumbled thoughts - and then a brilliant smile broke out across his face.

"I believe, Annelise, you have won."

◆ ◆ ◆

I closed the door to the room I had begun to think of as my own, and forced myself to take several deep breaths.

How I had sat in that room, with the tension crackling around us, and not reached out to touch him, I would never know.

It had been a beautiful evening, one that made it even harder to leave. I almost wished we had stayed on the bad terms we had been on that morning, just so I could leave feeling frustrated, rather than sad.

Who would have predicted it would be so hard to say goodbye to someone I had known for less than two weeks?

When my heart had finally returned to a rhythm that felt more normal, and I had managed to stop my mind reliving the moment he had spoken of love and family in this beautiful home, I realised I needed to leave.

Now.

If I left in the morning, it would surely be too painful. If I saw him again, I wasn't sure I would have the strength to leave - and now, alone in this room, I reminded myself that leaving was obviously the right thing to do. I needed to get on with my life, just as he needed to get on with his. Lives that never needed to cross paths, ever again.

I struggled to untie the borrowed dress, wishing Edith would magically appear again, but knowing if she did she would surely say something that would make me doubt myself.

My own dress was simpler to put on, and I was amazed how thin, how scratchy, how faded it seemed after the dresses I had been wearing. I gave myself a mental shake; that would teach me for becoming spoilt in such a short period of time. My own dresses had served me perfectly well before, and they would do again.

I could not take his coach without speaking with him, but I had planned to get a public coach before, and I thought it best I get used to normal life again, anyway. It wouldn't leave until the morning, but the night was thankfully dry, and so I could walk into the town and find somewhere sheltered to wait until I could be on my way home.

Home.

The thought brought tears to my eyes, and I wasn't sure if I was desperate to be there or never wanted to return.

I looked round the room, and reminded myself that I had arrived with nothing but this dress and thin cloak, and would leave with nothing but that.

Well, except maybe a broken heart.

When I was sure the house sounded quiet, I opened the bedroom door and softly walked to the top of the stairs. I carried my shoes, knowing they would make more noise than I could afford. As I paused on the top step, I wondered if I should leave a note, but I figured that Nicholas would realise where I had gone. It was only a few hours premature, anyway; this moment had always been coming.

I stepped onto the stair, and it creaked. My whole body froze; how had I not noticed the staircase was this loud?

I took another step, and another creak - and just as I was about to make a run for it and let the noise be damned, his door opened.

"Annelise?"

CHAPTER THIRTY-EIGHT

Nicholas

Although I had been in bed a while, I had not fallen asleep. No, my mind hummed with the revelations that had become apparent to me that evening.

Namely, how amazing it was that Annelise Edwards had turned down my offer of marriage.

And how I could not imagine my life without her in it.

I had sat up instantly when I heard a creak on the stairs, and the re-occurrence had caused me dash to my door. I did not know what I was expecting, but seeing her there, in the dress she had arrived in, made my heart stutter.

"Are you... leaving?"

She closed her eyes, and I could only just see her by the light from the candle in my hand. Then she nodded, and I felt my heart breaking.

"Please don't go." The words left my mouth, and I did not give myself time to think how I would feel if she rejected me again. Her eyes widened, and I took two steps towards her, lighting up her face with the flickering flame, as her mouth dropped open in shock.

"Stay," I repeated, emotion making my voice thick. "You... you could have everything. And you said no..."

"Nicholas-"

"No, please, listen. I thought you were saying no because you didn't... that it was something wrong with *me*. But I think-"

"There's nothing wrong with you," she whispered, and I almost dropped the candle in my rush to take her hand in mine. "But I come from nothing. I don't belong here."

"I don't care," I said, setting the candle down as carefully as I could with my shaking hands, and taking her other hand in mine. "I don't care where you came from, I don't care who your parents are, or whether they were married. I promise you, Annelise - I just don't want you to leave."

It was so hard to put myself out there, to let her see how much I wanted her to stay, even if I didn't truly understand it myself. I had never been this vulnerable in front of Bridgitte, I was sure - and yet she had hurt me more than any woman before her. And yet something about Annelise made me want to be vulnerable, to show her that I meant these words more than anything I'd ever said in my life.

"I don't want to leave," she whispered, and those words were enough for me. I took her head in my hands, revelling in the feel of her skin beneath my fingertips, and our eyes met for a moment in the dying light of the candle, before I lowered my lips to hers.

She responded instantly, her lips warm and soft, her body pressing closer to me, and all thoughts of feigning disinterest were long forgotten. As my tongue dipped between her lips, my hands moved from her head, down to her waist, pulling her closer to me. I could feel the heat from her body, and I fancied I could feel the quickening pace of her heart against mine.

Pausing to let her take a breath, I moved my lips to her cheek, the shell of her ear, the nape of her neck. Wherever there was bare flesh, my lips wanted to be - and she let out a moan that only spurred me on.

A door shut somewhere below us, and we both froze, aware of our position, out here on the landing.

I was going to ask her to marry me again, that I knew - and so I felt no guilt at offering her my hand, and leading her into my bedroom.

She followed without faltering, and I tried to steady my erratic heartbeat by focusing on the warmth of her hand encased in mine.

She could have had everything, and she said no because she didn't think she was good enough.

That wasn't a rejection of me; that was a pure, misguided act that made me...

That made me love her even more.

The realisation hit me like a horse bolting from the stables, and in that moment I knew that I had never experienced love properly before.

CHAPTER THIRTY-NINE
Annelise

This was it, I was sure; the moment of no return.

We weren't married, and I had no idea if that was still an option - but there was no way I was going to walk away from this moment.

Nicholas stood there in a lawn shirt that was open at the collar, a smattering of dark hair upon golden skin peeking through. Just looking at him stood there, his ebony hair mussed where I had run my hands through it, made me feel a little shaky - and, as if he sensed that, he pulled me closer, using his body to support me while his fingers stroked down the side of my face. One paused on my lips, and I closed my eyes for a moment against the onslaught of emotion and sensation that I was currently experiencing.

"Annelise," he said, and my eyes fluttered

open. I could not resist the sound of my name on his lips. "I have never wanted anyone like I want you."

Oh.

I had not imagined to hear those words, and it made the fire within me burn hotter and brighter, wiping all thoughts from my mind.

Feelings I did not understand swelled up in my chest, and I tentatively let my hand roam up the solid planes of his chest, feeling the heat of his skin through the thin shirt. My fingers reached his bare skin, and I focussed on the feeling beneath my fingertips. When I reached the base of his throat he let out a breathy moan, and I felt the vibrations where the pads of my fingers touched his skin.

"Nicholas." I had nothing else to say, but as our eyes met, there was no need for further conversation. Our lips touched once more, and I felt the soft mattress against the back of my legs. I knew this should be setting off warnings in my mind, but all I could think was how right it felt to have my arms around Nicholas's broad back, to lie on this bed next to him and feel his tongue touching mine in a shocking display of desire.

This clearly must be what happened in the marriage bed - and all I could hope was that he realised how little I knew, of anything, and did not think badly of me for it.

One hand roamed down my side, feeling ticklish in some places and delicious in others, and paused as it found bare skin at the bottom of my dress. Slowly, tantalisingly so, his warm fingertips moved up the outside of my leg, skin that had not been touched by sunlight, let alone another person. I broke the kiss to focus on everything my body was feeling, but it all seemed too much as he whispered into my ear: "You are so beautiful, Annelise."

CHAPTER FORTY
Nicholas

She was a true beauty, laid out on the bed in her simple dress, the light from the fire highlighting the emotion in her eyes as they met mine.

I presumed she was an innocent, although it was hard to know what her mother might or might not have told her. I did not want to scare her away, but neither did I want to do something she did not understand.

"I want to be with you," I whispered. "To join together, as a man and wife do."

My fingers stroked the soft flesh on the outside of her thigh, and I watched as pleasure flitted across her face from that simple contact. "Yes," she said. "Yes, Nicholas, I want you..."

I renewed my attention on her lips, feeling like I could never get enough of her beautiful kisses, of her body writhing on the bed despite the fact that we were only kissing. Then, smiling as she let out an irritated sigh, I moved away slightly and pulled my shirt over my head, throwing it to the floor. She watched, eyes wide, without blinking, and then sat up, reaching up to run her hand from my neck down to where the laces of my trousers grazed my skin.

It was my turn to look in shock, and she blushed so prettily at her own daring.

Kneeling before her on the bed, I reached for the ribbons on her dress, wondering - and not for the first time - how women coped with having such complex garments to put on every day. But eventually hers too were on the floor, and she lay there simply in her shift, blushing and grinning in equal measure.

"I..." she said, reaching to take my hand, and I responded by pulling hers to my lips for a sweet kiss. "I have no idea what I'm supposed to do."

My heart burst at her honesty. Leaning to press a kiss to her lips, I gently maneuvered us so we were lying side by side. "I'll show you," I promised, my fingertips finding her hips and pulling her tight to me, where she could undoubtedly feel the effect she had on me.

"I trust you," she whispered, and the words brought a smile to my lips. I hoped I could be worthy of that trust.

For a few moments more we simply kissed,

letting our bodies press together through very little clothing, before I allowed my hands to move across her body. Gently I cupped her breast, feeling her moan against my skin, and then moved down, down until my fingers were once more on bare skin. Without getting her to sit up, I managed to remove the shift, and then she lay before me, with nothing to hide behind except that smile.

And although she looked embarrassed, it did not leave her face.

Without standing, I managed to divest myself of my own remaining clothes, until there was nothing between us at all.

"Beautiful," I reaffirmed, wishing I could see her in better light, not just the embers of the fire.

But there would be time for that, in the future; for now I felt a desire so strong I had to remind myself to slow down, to take things gently. She trusted me; I wanted to deserve that trust.

CHAPTER FORTY-ONE

Annelise

I gave myself up to him entirely, pushing away any thoughts of embarrassment at the fact that neither of us was wearing anything. At least the light was dim, and it would not be easy to see me blush.

Nerves swam in my stomach, but more than anything I just wanted to know what it felt like to be his - even if it were only for a night. He whispered sweet words in my ears that made me close my eyes and wish I could find something to say in return.

His fingers continued to wander my bare skin, and I let my hands travel until they tangled in his long, dark hair, keeping him close to me. I was a little embarrassed of how little I knew of this marriage act, but when his body pressed against me I felt him hot and wanting, and I tried to let instinct take over.

It could have been minutes or hours later, but I became aware of his body on top of me, encasing my whole being in his warmth. His fingers moved once more, lazily down from my throat, over one breast, then the other, then down, dipping between my legs in an action that made me blush even hotter than before. The look in his eyes was just as sinful, and as he moved his fingers in a way that made me gasp, I had to close my eyes and focus on those sensations.

If I stared into his eyes, I feared I might get lost in them forever.

Pleasure tingled through my body as he moved, awakening a feeling in the pit of my stomach that I had never known before. I could not name it, but as it built I knew I needed for him to continue.

And then he paused, pressing his lips to my ear once more, and whispered so delicately it made my skin prickle. "This may hurt, a little. But I promise, not for long."

I nodded, knowing that in this moment, I would not have said no to anything.

He moved slowly, and as we joined together I felt a sharp pain and bit my lip to avoid crying out. But he noticed, and for a moment we lay completely still, his lips against my ear, and I felt so many emotions I had to force myself to breathe slowly, in case I started to cry in earnest.

CHAPTER FORTY-TWO
Nicholas

I did not want to hurt her, but I knew of no way to avoid it, and so I held her and pressed my lips to her skin and waited in sweet torture until she relaxed around me.

My eyes met hers and she gave a little nod, and I pressed my lips to hers in a passionate kiss that had her arching up to meet me as I began to move.

It was like nothing I had known before. I tried to control myself, to make it as pleasurable for her as it was for me, but her body lit a fire in me that made thinking impossible. She gasped as I moved, then pulled my head down to kiss her, and I thought I would be happy to be lost in her kisses forever.

We moved together in a simple dance that was as old as time, and as her breathing became more frantic and she let out a moan of pure pleasure, I lost all self-control, my own release timing perfectly with hers.

CHAPTER FORTY-THREE
Annelise

I could not explain what had just happened, but for a second or two it felt like my vision was filled with stars. After a groan that did not help to slow my racing heart, he rolled off me, but stayed right by my side, pulling me closer so I was nestled in the crook of his arm.

A sigh escaped my lips as my limbs seemed to melt into the bed, exhausted and immobilised by this new experience. I had not known what I was letting myself in for, but I had certainly not imagined it could feel anything like this. The pleasure was one thing, one amazing thing, but as I felt Nicholas's arm pull me even nearer to him, I wondered if I had ever felt so close to another person in this world.

He hooked the blanket from the bottom of the bed with one foot, and placed it gently over us.

The thoughtful gesture made me smile; not only was I growing colder, but I was also increasingly aware of how much of my body was on display.

"Do you feel...all right?" he asked, pressing a soft kiss to the top of my head.

I smiled, and answered completely honestly. "I feel wonderful."

CHAPTER FORTY-FOUR
Nicholas

I pressed my lips to her shoulder, unable to hide my grin at her answer. She was wonderful, and I felt a bubble of happiness in my chest as I held her close. Our breathing slowly returned to its normal pace, but my smile did not fade. I could not believe that this evening had ended so wonderfully. And now, as I felt her drift asleep in my arms, I knew I never wanted to let her go.

CHAPTER FORTY-FIVE
Annelise

I awoke to the sound of the door opening, and for a moment I could not place where I was. The hangings on the bed were a deep red, instead of blue, and the fireplace was on the opposite side of the room.

Then I turned my head to see Nicholas's face beside mine, his mouth open, slack in sleep, his dark hair fanned out around his head, his body entirely bare beside me.

I jolted upright then, realising the blanket that we had fallen asleep under was somehow now wrapped around me alone, and the door was open.

My eyes met those of Nicholas's elderly servant - Harris, I thought his name was - and I felt my cheeks burn bright red.

For a moment silence hung in the air, and then he nodded in a stiff bow, and closed the door behind him.

I lay back with a groan of embarrassment, taking only the briefest of peeks at Nicholas's sculpted, naked form before ensuring we were both covered by the blanket.

"Nicholas," I muttered, reaching out to touch his arm. "Nicholas?"

His eyes blinked open, and the smile that spread across his lips at the sight of me was one I would not forget in a long time.

"Good morning," he said, and before I could say a word his fingers were threading their way through the hair at the back of my neck, and he was pulling me in for a sweet morning kiss.

Well, it was nice to know he didn't seem to regret last night, at least. I tried to forget that my body was a hair's breadth away from his, or that there were no clothes separating us, as I remembered why I had woken him.

"Someone just came in," I said. "Harris, I think? And he saw... us."

Nicholas chuckled, and I felt my brows knitting together. Did he not understand?

"Nicholas, we are wearing no clothes, we are in bed together, and someone saw us!"

He pushed himself up so his head was

propped up on his fist, and took my hand in the other. Such innocent contact still made my heart race, my cheeks blush, even after what we had done last night.

"Annelise," he said, lifting my fingers to his lips in the lightest of kisses. "I want to marry you. It doesn't matter if Harris saw you in my bed."

I swallowed, my eyes going wide. "You- you do? Even in spite of..."

"In spite of everything. In spite of the fact that you beat me at chess-" He pressed a kiss to the hollow of my neck and I could not help the gasp that escaped my lips. "And you go out in the rain far too much-" His lips grazed the skin between my breasts, and I giggled at his words even as I moaned at the contact. "And you shouted at my doctor..."

I rolled my eyes at that one, and he pressed his lips to my stomach, before pulling me so that I was beneath his gorgeous body.

"It doesn't matter?" I asked, and I didn't know if I was referring to Harris walking in or my inferior status.

"Nothing matters," he said with a smile. "Nothing except the two of us, in this room."

My heart felt like it melted at those words, seeping through me with a delicious heat that made me forget that there was anything outside these four walls. I forgot about the differences between us, forgot about all the excellent reasons I had for turning down his marriage proposal, forgot about the fact that he had offered his hand to save my reputation, not because he was in love with me.

And even though I had not yet accepted this second offer of marriage, as we moved together once more I knew in my heart that I would.

❖ ❖ ❖

After Nicholas went to my room to fetch me a dress to wear, we managed to leave the bedroom, strolling down the stairs hand-in-hand. I found myself looking at him, and when our eyes met we both grinned like fools.

What was this feeling? I knew I was happy, knew despite the tiredness and slight soreness I was feeling, that this was the best morning I could remember.

But could it be... love? I baulked at the word, knowing I had never been in love before, and so how would I know it if I was? But when he paused at the bottom of the stairs to give me a searing kiss, I thought this might well be what it felt like to be in love.

"I'll meet you in the great hall," he said, releasing my hand with a soft kiss to the knuckles. "I just need to fetch something from the library."

I nodded, and watched him go before turning and walking away myself, feeling like the ground was air beneath my feet. It was as though I were living in some perfect dream, and Nicholas was giving me a way to never wake up from it.

Voices in the great hall made me pause before I entered, and although I didn't mean to eavesdrop, I couldn't help myself when I heard my name mentioned.

"Annelise?"

"Yes! Apparently Harris walked in on them together, in bed, if you know what I mean!"

"Of course I know what you mean, you stated it obviously enough." That was Edith's voice, I was sure, and I tried to remember Nicholas's reassurances that it did not matter that everyone would know, as my stomach churned in embarrassment.

"Well, apparently she's naught but the daughter of a maid and a gardener! One of the kitchen boys overheard her in the garden, talking to Mr Stockwall. Her mother used to work here, if you can believe it!"

I wished I could walk away, but Nicholas would be meeting me here any moment, and I had no good reason to not eat breakfast with him.

"I don't think that makes a blind bit of difference," Edith said.

"Really?" Another voice joined the mix now. "Lord Gifford comes from a long line of nobility. You think if he marries a maid's daughter, it will be accepted?"

"Marriage?" the first voice spluttered, and I felt my heart pounding in my ears. "Who was talking of marriage?"

"Well, he's got her in his bed, in his home, where everyone will know about it. Surely marriage has been offered?"

I wanted to hear the response as much as I dreaded it, but I heard the library door shut and knew I could not have Nicholas find me like this. With a deep breath, I pushed open the doors and walked to my seat with my head held high, as the three of them scurried away.

I would not let them see how much their words had hurt me - even if I could not erase them from my mind.

CHAPTER FORTY-SIX
Nicholas

I did not notice, when I sat down to break my fast, that she was quiet. Perhaps because I was so hungry, after losing my interest in the meal the night before and being active for so much of the night - and so I tucked into the meal placed before me. It took several minutes to realise she was barely eating, and that the conversation that was normally so easy was absent.

"Are you well?" I asked, and she nodded, giving a small smile that I did not totally believe.

I continued to eat, getting lost in my own thoughts. Perhaps she was in pain, from the night before, I thought - or simply contemplating how fast everything had changed. Perhaps she had regrets, or was ashamed for lying with me when we weren't yet wed. If that were the case I wished to ease her worries - I had no issues with marrying in great haste, if she would prefer - although if she wished to wait for a new dress to be made and guests to be invited, I was content with that too.

The wedding did not worry me at all; now that I knew I wanted her to be my wife, that I loved her, the marriage was all I needed.

When I looked over at her again, and realised her heart was not bursting with joy like mine was, I started to feel a little uneasy.

"Annelise," I murmured, smiling at the blush that spread across her cheeks. "Are you sure nothing is bothering you?"

She shook her head. "No, I'm quite well," she insisted. "Tired, is all."

I could not suppress a smile at that, the reasons for her tiredness flashing through my mind. "You should rest," I said, reaching out to touch her hand. "And then later, we can talk."

I knew there were things we needed to discuss, after putting the cart before the horse last night where the wedding was concerned. But I also knew it was going to be difficult to not sweep her into my arms and cloister us in the bedroom for the next few days, now I knew the joy that was to be had in her embrace.

CHAPTER FORTY-SEVEN
Annelise

I tried to smile, but my mind was a mess of emotions and half-thought ideas, and I knew I needed to be away from his beautiful smile and his gentle touch to process this information properly.

And so I took him up on his suggestion of a rest, and pushed my plate away from me, hunger the last thing on my mind. As I turned to leave through the same door at which I had heard those terrible words, he called my name.

"Annelise?" I turned my head, and saw a guilty looking smile on his face as he pushed his chair backwards and took two steps towards me.

"Can I..." He reached forward, cupping his hand around my head, tipping my face backwards slightly until it would be so easy for him to kiss me.

And then he waited, waited for my approval,

waited for me to do or say something.

I knew I needed to get out of that room, but his lips so close to mine were an invitation I could not refuse. Standing on tiptoes to close the gap between us, our lips met in a passionate kiss that was almost enough to burn all my worries away.

"Sleep well," he said, a brilliant smile upon his lips as we broke apart. "I'll see you later."

I nodded, my mind too muddled from the kiss to think of a response, and walked out of the room and up the stairs without thinking where my feet were taking me.

He was of a noble line.

I was the daughter of a maid.

It would not be accepted.

The words span round in my head like a sycamore seed in the wind, making me dizzy as I contemplated their meaning. The words were cruel, but the women behind them had been right; our marriage would make Nicholas a laughing stock. He had spent time with the King and Queen of England; what on Earth would they think to a noble lord marrying the bastard daughter of a maid-come-washer-woman?

I leant against the door of the Blue Room, my head in my hands, tears threatening to fall. Last night, this morning, it had been perfect; but one perfect night did not erase the fact that Nicholas was offering me an amazing life - at great cost to himself.

He liked me, I was fairly sure of that; he enjoyed my company, and our bodies had certainly seemed compatible. But he must not have been thinking past the elation of our coupling last night, to what people would say and think about our marriage.

He would be shunned, I was sure of it, and I would receive far crueller barbs than the ones I had suffered in secret this morning.

Nicholas was a good man, and now we had acted as man and wife, I was sure there was no way he would leave me.

So I would have to leave him.

For both our sakes.

There was no time to change, and so I had to hope he would forgive me taking the dress. I needed to be gone before he noticed my absence - and before I changed my mind. One look into his green eyes and I knew I would be lost forever - but how much would I hate myself in years to come, when this man that I had come to love was being shunned by those he had always known as his peers?

Acceptance was everything in this world, and he had it. I could not be the one to make it crumble around him.

I managed to get down the stairs this time without being discovered, but as I passed the library I realised there was one more thing I had to do. Pleased to find a quill and parchment lying on the desk, I penned a brief note that could not possibly encapsulate my feelings, then ran through the door before any tears could fall on the page.

The coach would surely have gone by now, but I could not take a carriage without him knowing, let alone prepare one for travel. I could borrow a horse, though - his stable had several - and leave it at a coach house in London, and send him word of where to collect it. I knew I was taking so many liberties, but I also knew if I did not leave now, I would be persuaded otherwise.

Two horses were saddled, and although I did not know who they were for, I chose the calmest looking one of the two and led it from the stables before I scrambled on to its back. I had never been the most competent horse rider, but I had ridden a handful of times before and hoped the horse knew what it was doing better than I did.

"Come on, girl," I whispered, tears dripping from my cheeks. "Let's go."

CHAPTER FORTY-EIGHT
Nicholas

I read the newspaper while enjoying a second helping of food, wondering how long I should let Annelise sleep for. I was keen to talk to her about when we should wed, and when we should travel to London to collect the rest of her belongings. I was well aware that there were other things I was keen to do as well, but after her reticence at breakfast I knew I needed to hold back a little. She had lit a fire in me that I could not quite control, and when images flashed through my mind of her last night, in my bed, in my arms, face contorted in pleasure... well, it took a great deal of effort not to go and find her.

I considered attempting to read, but knew my mind was too wild to focus, and so I decided on a walk around the grounds. The weather was mercifully dry, and I fancied the lush greenery might calm me a little.

When I walked past Mr Stockwall, carefully planting a sapling in the soil, I smiled and wished him good morning. There was so much I wanted to say to him about his daughter, about how wonderful she was, about how I loved her and wanted to make her happy - but that was not my place. Not yet. He had only been her father for a day or two - I could not suddenly declare my intentions as a son-in-law.

But the thought that she would be living so close to the only member of her family left was a good one, and the smile stayed on my face as I stretched my legs and breathed in the fresh smell of wet grass.

When I was sure it must be approaching lunchtime, I climbed the stairs and reminded myself that I was only checking on Annelise - certainly not climbing into bed with her. There would be plenty of time for that, when she was ready and rested. Opening the door to my chamber, I was disappointed to see the bed made and the blankets unruffled. I supposed it would make sense that she would feel more at home in the Blue Room, but I hoped from now on we would have one chamber; this chamber. I had no interest in being a husband in a separate bedroom any more, no matter what my feelings had been on the matter in the past.

Upon opening the door to the Blue Room, I was met with a similar sight, and my stomach began to churn with a nervousness I did not fully understand.

Surely, she had come to find me, or gone for a walk in the gardens, or...

I tried to persuade myself that all of those options were equally likely, but in the back of my mind I could not help but remember that she had been ready to walk away last night, without saying goodbye; would she really do it again, after the night we had spent together?

I worried I did not really know her well enough to answer that question.

I checked the hallway, the great hall, and was about to head outside when I noticed the door to my library was ajar. I always kept it closed; perhaps she had simply gone in there to find me?

When I saw a piece of folded parchment on the desk, with my name on the front, my heart sank.

Dear Nicholas,

Thank you for everything. I am so sorry I could not stay, but I have realised our marriage would risk you losing the respect and place in society you deserve. I cannot be the one to cause you that pain.

Yours,

Annelise

I sank into the chair, holding the parchment so tightly it trembled in my hand.

Yet again I had been rejected, yet again she had left me.

But as tears threatened to well up in my eyes, I could not ignore the truth: she had done it to protect me. It was misguided, certainly - I did not care what society thought, and once we were married, I doubted anyone would care about her heritage for more than a month or two at most.

For all that I had not known her long, I felt that there was honesty in these words.

And so I had to get her back.

Grabbing a cloak I had slung over the back of a chair the previous day, I dashed from the room. She couldn't have been gone long - why, I'd only seen her two hours earlier. Would she have taken a coach? A horse? Or walked? A quick visit to the stables should ascertain that, I thought, as my hand reached the front door to yank it open.

And there, stood before me wearing a red dress and a bemused look was yet another member of my family who would have no qualms interfering in my life.

"Mary!"

"Nicholas!" She smiled, and pulled me into a

brief hug before pushing me away to look at my face. "We need to talk."

Somehow I found myself being maneuvered back inside by my little sister, away from the urgent course I had set myself on.

"Mary," I said, between gritted teeth. "Please do not take offence at this, but I do not have time. I'm delighted to see you, but-"

"Aunt Eleanor stopped by, on her way to see cousin Richard," she said, as if that explained everything.

And I supposed, in some ways, it did.

CHAPTER FORTY-NINE
Annelise

I could not ride with much haste, riding in a far more elaborate dress than I had ever worn atop a horse before, but when an hour passed and there was not a rush of hooves behind me, I began to calm down.

There was no reason he should want to come after me, I told myself. He had not declared his love, nor I mine - even though I was becoming more and more certain that this ache in my heart was indeed true love.

I passed through a small town, wishing I had money with me to buy at least something to drink, or some food. I was sorely regretting not eating at breakfast, even though my stomach would not have accepted it.

With a sigh, I continued on, down the quiet road that led to London. It would not be the first day I had gone hungry, and I doubted it would be the last - but after so many days of good food, my body was crying out for sustenance.

CHAPTER FIFTY

Nicholas

"Nicholas," she said, sounding much older than her twenty-three years. I supposed marriage had matured her, but I struggled to think of her as anything but the little brat who would steal my toy soldiers and cry to Father if I beat her in a game. "I understand you have feelings for some girl who has been staying here."

"Yes." What was the point in denying it? At any moment I was going to have to rudely push past her and jump on a horse, as every second that passed made it more likely I would never see Annelise again. I had no idea where she lived in London, other than that it was near the Thames - and that hardly narrowed things down.

"And she is the daughter of a maid, correct?"

"I don't care-"

"But you should, Nicky!" she said, throwing her arms in the air in exasperation and reminding me for a moment of our mother. "You will make a fool of yourself. No, listen, I don't mean to be harsh. But that business with Bridgitte was damaging enough - and I'm sure you were hurt into the bargain too. I know it wasn't your fault, but think of the scandal if you marry a girl of low parentage! You couldn't present her at court, she wouldn't know how to behave, how to run a household like this. Now, I understand men have certain needs..."

"Mary!" The words leaving my sister's mouth shocked me into a blush, although I guessed as she was a married woman, I should not have been so surprised.

She blushed too, but pushed on. "But you don't have to marry a girl because you're interested in her affections. You can be discreet, you can-"

"I'm in love with her," I said, feeling the emotion strengthen as I said the words. "Mary, this is not some dalliance, no matter what our aunt might say. I don't care about her parentage; I don't care if she has not a shilling to her name. She is good, she is kind, and she understands everything I feel. I am in love with her, and I cannot imagine having another woman as my wife."

Her mouth dropped at that, and I wondered if I had ever spoken so honestly to her before. For a long time I had felt I had to protect her from the evils of the world, as her elder brother - and then she had married, and I heard from her by letter a handful of times a year.

"I didn't realise you felt that way," she said, and the blush on her cheeks made me wonder if perhaps she understood more of true love than I realised.

"So if you'll excuse me," I said, feeling like the time was disappearing like sand through my fingertips, "I must go and find her - before it's too late."

She did not encourage me, but she did not say anything to stop me either, and so I raced from the room to the stables. A bay mare was definitely missing, and I did not have time to saddle up my mount. Luckily, I had ridden Lancelot many times before bareback, and so he adjusted easily and we were away, cantering at a speed that I hoped would far outstrip Annelise and her mare.

There was one main route to London, and I hoped she knew where she was going - else finding her would be a lot more of a challenge.

As Lancelot's hooves pounded into the ground, I let my mind contemplate the words Mary had said. If she'd said them a few days previously, I believed I may well have accepted them; thought that my feelings for Annelise were merely an infatuation, and that any association with her would be trouble for our family name.

But then I had realised who she really was,

how truly good she was, and my heart was lost.

And now I did not think it would matter who her parents were, or where she came from, or what she had done - I could not be without her.

I only hoped I could make her see that; make her feel the same way.

CHAPTER FIFTY-ONE
Annelise

As I approached a river, I slowed down, feeling the need to stop for a moment. With little grace, I slid from the horse (who I had named Sugar in my mind) and patted her soft nose.

"Thank you," I whispered, leading her to the water where she gratefully drank. I stretched my limbs carefully, feeling an ache where I had sat in the saddle for too long. My thoughts dangerously wandered to what Nicholas would be doing right now. Would he have found my note? Would he be regretting our actions the previous night? Or just feel relief that the whole incident was over, without him publicly declaring anything for me?

Despite the chill in the air, I sat on the grass for a while, taking in deep breaths of the spring breeze. All around us, plants were ready to break into flower and I hoped that the positivity of the season would not be lost in the sadness that I felt.

I wanted Nicholas to be happy - but I had also wanted the dream he had painted, the one of us married and together until the end of our days.

I did not raise my head as I heard hooves approaching, too lost in my misery to want to pass the time of day with a stranger - until I heard feet on the ground instead of hooves, and my head snapped up.

"Annelise," he said, striding towards me as though he had not just dismounted from a cantering stallion - who had joined Sugar by the water.

"Nicholas! I- You shouldn't- I-"

He took my hands in his, and the words disappeared from my mouth as his eyes met mine.

"I understand," he said. "I understand why you left, I understand what you thought, but I'm here to tell you that I do not feel that way."

My hand reached out to stroke his cheek as tears filled my eyes. "No, Nicholas, you don't understand, I overheard-"

"Annelise Edwards," he said, interrupting my admission with his strong voice. "I am in love with you. I don't think I have made that clear, so I want to now. I asked you to marry me out of concern for your reputation, and you said no. But I am not asking now to preserve your name, or because of a sense of duty, or even because we have lain together."

In his beautiful, fine clothes, he knelt down on the wet grass, and as rain began to fall from the gathering clouds above, he said the most beautiful words. "I am asking you to be my wife because I am in love with you. Because I can imagine no other woman by my side and in my bed. I am asking you because I think I need you to be whole, to be the person I am supposed to be."

"Are... Are you sure?" I asked, cursing myself for questioning this but needing to know there would be no regrets before I declared my feelings too.

"I am positive," he said, love blazing his eyes, and so I knelt on the floor with him, tears filling my vision.

"I love you, Nicholas," I said. "Yes. Yes, I will marry you, if you are sure you want me."

"I want every part of you," he said, and although the rain began to fall in earnest, soaking our clothes and hair and skin with its cool touch, his lips upon mine lit a fire that I doubted could ever be extinguished.

And I never wanted it to be.

CHAPTER FIFTY-TWO
Nicholas

I realised before she did that the rain had soaked us to our skin, and memories of her terrifying fever came flooding back.

"We must get out of this weather!" I said, and she nodded, following me as I took her hand and helped her back onto the mare she had borrowed.

"Follow me," I said, vaulting onto Lancelot and nearly slipping off thanks to the rain that poured from the sky. Luckily, we weren't far from a little town, and I rode as fast as I could with Annelise still keeping up. I wished I could slide her onto my horse and hold her tight, protect her from some of the rain, but we needed to bring both horses back, and this seemed the quickest way.

With a quick glance behind me to check Annelise was watching, I veered off to the left and jumped off outside a small inn where I had stayed through some terrible weather or the need to re-shoe a horse on previous journeys to London. I raced over to her, helping her dismount the horse - who she affectionately patted on the nose - before tossing a coin to a young lad and asking him to take them round to the stable. I knew they'd be well taken care of here, and my priority was getting Annelise inside, out of this storm.

I took her by the hand, revelling in the feeling of it inside my much larger one, and shoved open the heavy wooden door.

The heat from the roaring fireplace hit us like a tidal wave, and for a moment I basked in it, feeling the water dripping steadily from every part of me, onto the rush-covered floor.

"Oh!" exclaimed the innkeeper, behind the bar, at the sight of us. "Oh, my lord!" He recognised me, I presumed, for I did not think my status was particularly obvious in such wet apparel.

"Do you have a room, sir?" I asked, wanting nothing but to ensure Annelise did not catch a chill again. "For my wife and I?"

The words weren't yet true, but they would be as soon as I could make them so - and the innkeeper did not need to know that.

"Of course, my lord, right this way."

We followed him, hand-in-hand, up the rickety staircase, and into a simple chamber with a decent-sized bed and a blissful fire that almost matched the one downstairs.

"Many thanks," I said, offering him a few coins. "Would a bath, and a hot meal, be possible?"

He looked in wonder at the coins in his hand, and nodded with a toothless grin. "Of course m'lord. I'll send it up as soon as it's ready, and have the bath and hot water brought up to you now."

"You are most kind," I said, and he tipped a bow before walking backwards from the room.

I turned to a silent Annelise, concern in my eyes and a hunger in my heart. Our hands were still entwined, and I could feel how cold she was to the touch - as was I.

"You called me your wife," she said, and I saw a smile playing on her soft lips.

"You will be soon," I said with a shrug.

"Wife."

I nodded, then reached to her cloak. "We need to get out of these wet clothes, before both of us are too ill to say our wedding vows."

She blushed, but nodded, and I untied the cloak, leaving it in a heap on the floor, before turning her round and beginning to unlace the back. I could not resist dipping my head to kiss the back of her neck, my wet hair trailing on her bare skin and making her wince slightly.

"Sorry," I whispered, loosening the dress until it could be easily removed.

"It's fine," she whispered, her voice catching as she ended with another word; "Husband."

She turned to face me, dressed in just her wet shift, the light from the fireplace catching the fire in her eyes, and I felt my heart jumping erratically in my chest. To call her my wife had felt extraordinary; but to be called her husband was something else entirely.

I could see it then, in her eyes; see the love she had spoken of, see the desire, see the concern.

"You need to take your wet clothes off too," she whispered, and with an endearing blush that the fireplace did not hide, she reached out and unbuttoned my cloak, adding it to the heap on the floor. Then she worked down the buttons of my shirt, her delicate fingers barely touching my skin but leaving a blazing pathway wherever they went.

It was a blessed relief to have the wet shirt off my back and on the floor, but even more so was the feel of her hand, pressed against the muscles of my stomach. I watched her for a moment, and she tentatively moved her fingers across my skin, before a knock at the door startled us both.

"You can go behind that screen," I said, and she scuttled away, while I went to answer the door. I did not really care that I wore no shirt - there was no way on Earth I was putting that wet piece of material back on, so whoever was delivering the bath would have to cope with me being half undressed.

Two lads carried the bath, while two maids carried pails of hot water, disappearing twice to refill them before the bath was full. After thanking them for their trouble - with another coin each for good measure - I shut the door behind them and called Annelise out.

"This should help warm us up," I said with a smile, wishing the moment between us had not been interrupted. I did not want to scare her, but by God did I want to see her without that shift on. It left very little the imagination anyway, and of course I had seen her naked once before - but in very poor light, and with far too much blanket around us.

"May I?" I asked, my hands reaching her hips and ruching the fabric up a little.

She bit her lip, then nodded, and I lifted it over her head in one fell swoop.

My eyes widened as she reached over to unlace my trousers, feeling the evidence of my desire for her straining against the fabric. But she did not comment, and for a moment we stood in front of the roaring fire, surrounded by our sodden clothes, with silly smiles on our faces.

And then I offered her my hand, and helped her in into the bathtub, before sliding in behind her.

CHAPTER FIFTY-THREE

Annelise

Although no vows had been said, as I sat between his legs in the small bath tub, feeling his hands stroke through my wet hair, I finally felt as though he was mine, and I was his. I leaned into the warmth of his touch as his fingers kneaded into my shoulders, and found my hands stroking up and down his muscled legs.

It felt like a dream, yet again, but the words he had said to me, out in the rain, started to make it feel real.

He loved me.

I loved him.

I gasped as his fingers were replaced by his lips, and soft kisses were rained down upon my skin.

"Nicholas," I sighed, his arms wrapping round my waist and pulling me closer to him. The water was cooling rapidly, despite the fire beside us, and I knew if we stayed in too long it would be as cold as the rain we had been soaked with - but his body felt so good against mine, and it was hard to think straight enough to voice these concerns.

"Annelise," he said, and I could hear the smile in his voice. "Let's get out, before we freeze again."

I nodded, blushing at the sight of his naked form as he scrambled out and offered me a hand, and then a towel. On top of the towels, one of the servants had left a hairbrush, and he toyed with it for a moment before glancing at me, my hair tangled and dripping onto the floor.

"May I?" he asked, and I nodded, sinking into the seat by the fireplace. He was so gentle, even though I knew the wind and rain had made my hair untameable, and I barely felt it as he pulled the brush through my hair over and over again. It felt hypnotic, as the warmth of the fire soothed my aching muscles and his hands repeated that delicate motion. And every now and then his fingers would graze against my neck, or my bare shoulders, and I would feel a frisson of excitement running through my whole body.

He was mine.

I was his.

And we were completely alone in this room with a very fine bed.

"There we go," he said softly, breaking my reverie. "I think all the knots are out."

I smiled, and reached to squeeze his hand. "Thank you, Nicholas."

A tap on the door made me jump, but he simply grinned and pointed towards the screen, which I disappeared behind again. He did not seem concerned about answering the door wrapped in a towel and nothing else, even though my cheeks were aflame just at the thought.

Once he had closed the door, I scurried out, picking up our wet clothes and hanging them from the mantelpiece in front of the fire. They were all we had, and they would need to be dry for us to redress and return back to Marvale.

To return home.

Set upon a tray were two steaming hot dishes of stew, and two goblets of wine, and my stomach rumbled in anticipation. I glanced at his ebony hair, wanting to brush it like he had mine, but knowing I needed food before doing anything else.

For a few moments we ate in silence, letting the hot meal warm us through after our adventure in the rain. Soft glances were shared, and a few smiles, before either of us spoke.

"So, my sister arrived, not long after you left."

My eyebrows rose. "Oh?"

"She wanted to make sure I wasn't making a mistake."

My heart sank. Just when I had begun to believe he could be mine, there was another family member who was dead set against us being together?

"Oh?" was all I managed to say, taking a sip of wine while I waited for his response.

"And I assured her I was not. And that I would not entertain the thought of marrying any woman who was not you."

"Oh."

"I just wanted you to know, Annelise," he said, his eyes seeming to burn as they met mine, his fingers reaching to make contact with my knee. "I don't want you to try to run away again. I want to get married as soon as we possibly can - and I don't give a damn who thinks otherwise."

I nodded, taking a moment to formulate my response.

"I don't want to cause a rift with your family," I said, then saw the panic in his eyes. "But I don't want to run away, either. Nicholas," I said putting my hand atop his. "I promise you, I won't leave you again."

"I won't leave you either," he said, a smile emerging on his face.

"Can I brush your hair?" I asked, the desire to do so overwhelming me, and his eyes widened slightly, before he nodded, pushing his empty bowl away and shuffling down in the chair slightly so I could reach the top of his head.

I lay my hands on the crown of his head first, feeling a strange sense of intimacy in the act, before taking the brush and running it slowly through his hair. It was nowhere near as tangled as mine had been, but the brush did snag in places and I tried to be as gentle as he had. It shone in the firelight as I brushed it, running my hands through it occasionally and grinning as he let out a moan.

"That feels good," he said. "I haven't had someone brush my hair in a very long time."

"Have you ever grown a beard?" I asked, letting one hand moved from his hair to his chin, feeling the coarse evidence of a recent shave. It surprised me how bold I had become, but now that we have spoken the words of love and promised each other forever, I could not resist letting myself explore a little.

"Once or twice," he said, closing his eyes as I continued my machinations. "I don't think it suited me."

"I like being able to see your face," I said, then blushed.

He turned, then, so fast I dropped the hair brush. "I like to see yours, too."

Taking hold of my face in both hands, his lips pressed to mine in a kiss that began so sweetly, so gently, but so quickly morphed into something else entirely.

The towels that had been wrapped around us fell to the ground, but neither of us noticed. My hands twisted in his hair, undoing all my hard work in brushing it, and his moved to my waist, moving us backwards until we fell onto the bed. His kisses made me feel breathless, and while my head swirled he pressed his lips to my neck, my collar bone, the swell of my breast.

"Nicholas," I panted, using the grip I had on his hair to encourage his head upwards, until our lips crashed together once more. I needed him like I needed air to breathe, and with every touch of his fingers to my body I was reminded that he wanted to marry me.

"My love," he whispered against my neck, and my eyes fluttered closed. I felt a swell of emotions rising up inside me, as lust warred with contentment at the words he spoke.

Tears threatened to overwhelm me at the realisation that I never had to be alone again. This beautiful man would be there when I went to sleep, when I woke up, when I was celebrating life's joys or mourning life's losses.

He would be there.

And as we joined together frantically, as though we could never get enough of each other, and shouted one another's names, tears I could not hold back began to fall.

"Annelise?" he said, breathless and naked next to me. "What ails you?"

I shook my head with a smile. "Nothing at all, my love. I'm just... happy."

He gathered me to his chest as our breathing began to slow and our hearts stopped racing quite so fast.

With a kiss pressed to the top of my head, he murmured: "So am I."

CHAPTER FIFTY-FOUR
Nicholas

Four weeks it had taken, to arrange a wedding that Mary had deemed was suitable for my rank. I would have married Annelise without a priest, would have said the words in front of a witness and been done with it.

But Mary had stayed, and Mary had insisted, and like little sisters so often did, Mary had got her own way.

There was a secret part of me, however, that was quite pleased to be having a more elaborate wedding. Not for me - I really did not care either way - but for Annelise. For her to have the chance to have a new, beautiful gown, and to be seen as the lady of the Manor in front of more than just a couple of witnesses - I thought that was an event she should not miss out on.

With Mary staying, we had not been able to share my chamber as I had planned. Whether we felt it or not, we were not yet married, and there were certain proprieties that had to be observed - especially in front of one's sister.

And so I had dutifully said goodnight to Annelise at the top of the stairs every one of those nights, with a chaste kiss and a sweet word.

And then tiptoed into her bedchamber as soon as the house had grown quiet.

We giggled beneath the blankets at our subterfuge, before spending long and glorious nights getting to know each other in every way possible. And although I longed for Annelise to be my wife in truth, without Mary seeing fit to play chaperone in my own house - she did not seem to take my hints as to whether her husband and children might be missing her - sneaking around was not too terrible.

When Mary commented on how tired we both looked at breakfast, I was afraid we had been caught out - but Annelise lied so smoothly about the sound of foxes in the grounds keeping her awake, that I had to stop myself staring at her in awe as I attempted to agree that the noise had indeed kept me awake from my own bedchamber.

CHAPTER FIFTY-FIVE
Annelise

I had spent the last four weeks getting to know Nicholas, and Mary, and this beautiful house better than I had in the fortnight I had been there already. I could not quite believe it had only been a fortnight; that my life had changed so irrevocably in that time.

It was two days after we returned from that inn that I went to find Rupert Stockwall. When we had last spoken it was full of goodbyes, and promises to write; now, I had news to share with him that would allow us to have a much closer relationship - if he truly wished us to.

It was a dry day, and as usual he was out in the gardens. This time he was tending to fruit trees, which thankfully did not seem to require him to kneel on the floor so often.

"Good afternoon!" I called out as soon as I

was in earshot, and I was rewarded with a smile as he made his way down the hill of the orchard towards me.

"Annelise! I thought you were away back to London," he said, looking pleased that I was here. That seemed like an auspicious start, at least.

"There has been a slight change of plan," I said, wondering how you explained that your whole life had been turned on its head.

"Oh?"

"This will... this will sound rather odd, I'm sure, but there is no other way to say it! I am to marry Nicholas - Lord Gifford." Saying his title made it seem all the less real; in my mind he had been just Nicholas, almost from the moment I had known his name.

His eyes widened, and I saw the shock flit across them. "I am as surprised as you," I reassured him. "But it does mean that I shall be staying here. At Marvale."

He nodded. "And you're... you're happy about this marriage? You aren't..." He licked his lips nervously, seeming to be struggling to find the right words. "You are marrying him of your own free will?"

"Oh, yes! I-" I blushed at the words I had not said to anyone other than Nicholas. "I have fallen in love with him."

"Oh! Well, then that is truly wonderful. And we shall be able to see other often, if you are living here! Although, I suppose, with you being a Lady..."

I could see where this particular conversation was going, and I cut him off. "I would love to see you as often as possible. And you can come to dinner, and lunch, and..." I was getting carried away with the idea of having a father, without thinking whether he would want those things - but I saw his face light up as I spoke, and so I let my fears settle.

"Lady Gifford," he said, a smile on his face. "Fancy that!"

"You know," I said, linking my arm with his as we walked towards the house. "I can't really believe it can possibly be true - but somehow it is!"

❖ ❖ ❖

It rained incessantly for three days, and on the fourth I insisted that I could cope with the drizzle to make the journey back to London to collect my belongings.

"At least let me accompany you," Nicholas said, lying next to me in my bed, speaking softly so Mary, whose chamber was down the hall, would not hear us.

"There's no need," I insisted, trailing my fingers across his bare arms, enjoying the feeling of his skin beneath my fingertips. "I will be back within the day."

"I don't like you being out of my sight," he said with a slight pout, and I laughed and pressed my lips to his, melting into him for a moment before remembering what I needed to say.

"I know. But I need to say goodbye to the place on my own. Please, trust me. I promise I'll come back."

His eyes shone and he nodded. "I do trust you. I'll just miss you."

"And I'll miss you. But you can spend some time with your sister, or working, or whatever it is you wish to do, and I will be back before you know it."

I could not tell him with complete honesty why I wished to go alone. I knew he would tell me it didn't matter, but I did not want him seeing the tiny home I had lived in. I did not want him pitying me, or worse, the visual reminder of how poor I was in my former life make him have second thoughts about our marriage. I did not truly think it would, but I certainly wasn't willing to risk it.

Rising early and breaking my fast quickly with Nicholas, I was on my way before the sun had properly risen. My journey was much more comfortable than when I had travelled here, or when I had tried to flee, for I had borrowed Nicholas's coach. His sister had loaned me some fabric and thread so I might sew on the journey to pass the time, but I spent most of it staring out the window at the rain-logged countryside and marvelling at how drastically my life had changed since I had made the journey here to find out about my mother's secrets.

London was as noisy and bustling as ever, and although the carriage drew the attention of a few of the market traders, we made it to our destination without too much hassle. I felt my stomach churning as I looked out of the window and saw the street where I had lived for so many years. It was unchanged, in the short weeks I had been away, even as I myself had changed so momentously.

"I shall be back shortly," I told the driver, who nodded, keeping a close eye on those around us who were interested in the carriage. It was a finer vehicle than we ever saw around these parts normally, and I knew not so long ago I would have been among the crowds gawping.

I half expected to see my mother rounding the corner as I put the key in the lock, before reminding myself that she had been gone for months now, and her face would not be appearing on London's streets.

Other than a layer of dust, our two little rooms were as they had always been. For a moment I stood and let the emotions of this place take hold of me; the bed where I had nursed Mother for many nights, before she had decided to travel to Marvale; the fire where we had cooked and kept warm; the neat pile of sewing that was waiting to be completed.

I sat on the bed, looking round at all we'd had to show for our life here, and felt my chest tightening. Hot tears poured from my eyes without warning, and I took several shuddering breaths as they fell on my hands and my fine, borrowed dress.

"I miss you so much," I whispered, speaking to my mother rather than the house. Her passing felt so much more real here, where we had spent all those days of our lives that would mean little to anyone else, but were everything to us.

Tears still rolling from my cheeks, I moved between the two rooms to gather up clothes, blankets, a couple of toys from my childhood and a bundle of letters Mother had saved. There was little else left, and I supposed I would not need most of it anymore, but I could not abandon these relics of our life, even as I abandoned this home.

With my bag full and my heart heavy, I

paused to press my fingers to the door frame where Mother had marked my growth every year with a notch in the wood.

"What if I'm making a terrible mistake?" I whispered to the cold, dusty air surrounding me. "What if I am an embarrassment, when I'm supposed to be lady of the manor?"

Of course, there was no response, and I wiped my eyes with a handkerchief and told myself to stop speaking to the air and get myself home.

Home.

I looked around and realised this was no longer my home; that would be Marvale, and I was falling in love with it a little more each day.

And just as I closed the door behind me, planning to give my new address to the neighbour just in case anyone happened to need to know where I was, the sun broke through the clouds and a sparkling shaft of sunlight illuminated our little home; a home that I hoped would give another family plenty of happy memories.

As the door closed, my heart found some peace at last.

❖ ❖ ❖

The day of our wedding dawned crisp and

mercifully dry. As romantic as our reunion in the rain had been, I thought I had seen enough rain until at least next year - and the effort Edith had gone to with my hair would surely be ruined by a downpour.

The banns had been read three weeks in a row at the surprisingly grand church in the local town, and no-one had come forth with any reason why we should not be married, and for that my heart sang with gratitude. I would not be prevented from marrying Nicholas, the man I loved, the man I had spent every night of the last four weeks with.

The man whose child I was fairly sure I was carrying.

It had been a feeling, to start with, that something was a little different. Then, when Edith had made a passing comment about the fact that I had not bled, I had blushed, not realising she would have taken note of such things - but when she explained how a woman might come to know she was with child, suddenly everything had started to make sense.

I found my hands gravitating to my stomach, imagining a life growing inside me. I had not mentioned my suspicions to Nicholas, in case I was wrong - but I knew I would feel much happier for so many reasons once we were truly wed, bound together until death.

There was a knock at the door, and I took one last look at myself in the glass - hair in ornate plaits down my back, my grey dress trimmed with so many beads it almost looked silver in the spring sunlight - before going to open it.

Mary stood there, a smile on her face. "Are you ready?" she asked, looking me up and down. "You look wonderful."

I nodded; "Thank you." I had not known how this sister of Nicholas's would treat me, knowing my status, knowing I was not the wife any of them would have wanted for the patriarch of the family. But a day or two in her company and I had begun to see similarities between the siblings, and when she had cheered me on as I beat Nicholas in another game of chess, I had felt I had gained an ally.

"Is Nicholas ready?" I asked shyly, and she rolled her eyes before looping her arm through mine.

"He's meeting us at the church, don't worry. It is traditional, after all, for the bride and groom to come from different households."

I blushed; there was nothing particularly traditional about this marriage, but I supposed if he wanted to meet me at the church, it would look a little more so to anyone looking on.

We stepped into the carriage, and as I looked

back Edith was giving me a wave and a smile from the window. Nerves fluttered in my stomach as I smiled back, and as the horses pulled away I took a deep breath.

"Are you nervous?" Mary asked, and I nodded.

"I was too, before my wedding day. But you're in a much better position than I was - you know Nicky well, and you love each other." She smiled softly, reaching out to give my hand a squeeze.

"Did you not know your husband?" I asked, and she shook her head.

"We had been pre-contracted for a long time, well before Father died. I met him over the years, perhaps once a year - but we definitely didn't know each other properly, or love each other."

"And do you now?" I asked, before thinking how forward the question was. But she did not hesitate long enough for me to take the words back, and when I heard her answer I was glad I had not been able to.

"I truly do," she said, a smile on her face and a blush in her cheeks. "I think I'm one of the lucky ones, to have fallen in love with the man who was chosen for me."

And I knew I was the luckiest of them all.

To marry a man who I had fallen so desperately in love with, to move to a place like Marvale and be catapulted from being a washerwoman to Lady Gifford - that was luck I could never have dreamed of.

"Today will be wonderful," Mary promised me, before a wicked smile spread across her face. "And after today, you won't have to sneak around after dark with my fool of a brother."

It was a good job that the carriage had stopped, for it saved me having to answer - although I was fairly sure my flaming red cheeks did most of the talking for me.

And we'd thought we'd been so clandestine!

CHAPTER FIFTY-SIX

Nicholas

I was surprised that I did not feel nerves as I stood outside the church, the March sunshine starting to feel almost warm on the back of my neck.

She had tried to run away twice, and yet I was sure as I stood and waited that she would be here today. The priest waited inside the door, and I took a moment to appreciate the peace of the day.

Once we had said our vows and bound ourselves together, we would celebrate with a feast and dancing back at Marvale with a few guests. There were not many to celebrate with, just those who would be witnessing our marriage at the church - Mary, of course, and her husband and sons who had travelled to meet her and see us wed. Aunt Eleanor, I hoped, and possibly my cousin. The only relative on Annelise's side would be Rupert, but he had beamed when I had asked him to attend, and so I was sure he would be comfortable among us.

Most of the guests were already inside, awaiting the bride, but I squinted into the sunlight as I saw a group walking down the pathway towards the front of the church.

A smile lit up my face at the sight of Aunt Eleanor, her arm entwined with her son's as she strode towards me.

"Aunt!" I said, reaching to embrace her, and then shook Richard's hand with a delighted grin. "Richard. It is wonderful to see you both." I did not let the smile slip, hoping that Eleanor would realise that today was not the day to make any comments about my choice of bride. She had said her piece, and the time had passed - I would not allow anything to ruin today.

"You are happy?" she asked, scrutinising my face.

"The happiest," I said, and she nodded.

"Very well," she said, motioning forwards to Richard. "We'll see you inside."

Behind her stood Mr Stockwall, dressed in the finest clothes I had seen him in, a smile on his face and a cap in his hand.

"My lord," he said, with a brief bow, but I

reached out to clasp his hand.

"Mr Stockwall," I said, hoping he could hear my sincerity. "I am so pleased you have come. And I know Annelise will be too."

He nodded. "I wouldn't have missed it for the world," he said. "I know I have not known her long, but I believe you two will be happy together."

"I do too," I said with a smile, and then the clattering of hooves alerted us to the arrival of the bride.

Rupert disappeared inside, and my eyes were fixated on the carriage door. Mary alighted first, taking the hand of the footman as she daintily stepped off, and then Annelise appeared, a vision in silver, her cheeks blushing a rosy red that made me wonder what was going through her mind.

Our eyes met, and for a moment the world stood still around us. And then Mary was hurrying her along, saying words that I barely paid attention to as she slipped inside and the priest joined us.

"You look beautiful," I told Annelise, and if it were possible she blushed even more.

"Are you both ready?" the priest asked, and we nodded.

"Do you both come here today, of your own free will, free of any other contracts of marriage?"

Again we nodded, and the priest blessed us before heading inside, where we followed him.

CHAPTER FIFTY-SEVEN

Annelise

The church was beautiful, I had thought that every time we had been - but now I forgot about everything around us, save for Nicholas. The faces of family and friends - almost solely his, of course - were a blur to me, and as I knelt with Nicholas before the priest, and repeated the words of the solemn vow that I knew I would keep for eternity, Nicholas was my only thought.

When Nicholas took my hand, and placed the blessed ring upon my finger, I felt an overwhelming urge to hold him close and never let go. But there would be time for that later; for now, the priest put the veil over our heads and recited words in Latin that I had little understanding of. I simply focussed on Nicholas's warm, strong body beside me, and the feel of the cold metal encircling my finger, reminding me that I was now to be somebody's wife.

Nicholas's wife.

When the air rushed in around us at the removal of the veil, Nicholas stood and offered me his hand, helping me up from the floor before pressing his lips to mine in a chaste kiss that promised of so much more.

"My wife," he whispered, as the church burst into applause.

"My husband."

CHAPTER FIFTY-EIGHT

EPILOGUE
Annelise

It had been innocuous enough, sat between piles of correspondence from a myriad of people, and as such it had taken me several months to actually find it.

Several months in which my body had grown heavier and heavier with child, and in which my heart had grown to love the man I had married even more each and every day.

It was on a day when he had insisted I rest, for my ankles were swollen and the babe was giving me little sleep at night, with its incessant little kicks, that I found the letter.

Despite the fact that I was now surrounded by so much luxury, I had not disposed of the items I had brought back with me from London. I had put them in a chest in our bedroom, and not thought about them again for a long while.

But when rest had become essential, and I had stopped being able to entertain guests, or visit the poor, or work with the local orphanage that I had taken an interest in, I had decided to go through those letters. Most were fairly mundane, letters my mother had kept from old friends who had told her of their everyday lives, and asked about hers.

But on that day, when I had reached for the pile of letters as I enjoyed a tray of sweet treats the cook kept bringing me, I had happened across one that bore my name.

Annelise Edwards

Well. It was not my name any longer, but it had been for the majority of my life. There was no address, and there was no doubting that it was my mother's handwriting.

I felt my heart jump in my chest. Why would she have written to me? We had lived our lives in such close proximity, what was there she would have chosen to write down instead of tell me?

As I broke the seal with my hands shaking, I was sure this must be about Rupert. What other secrets could she possibly have from me?

I scrunched my eyes closed for a moment, then forced them to open and focus on the writing in front of me. It was not dated, so I had no idea whether my mother had been ill or not when she had written it, but the script was neat and showed no sign of fragility in the writer.

My dear Annelise,

I do not know if you will ever read this, or whether I shall tell you this in person and burn this letter. But if you are reading it, I shall presume I am no longer of this world, and there are some things I should like you to know.

Firstly, you are my greatest accomplishment. Nothing in my life has made me prouder or happier than you, and I do not think you can fully understand that until you have a child of your own. I hope I can be there when that happens, to support you and meet the future members of our family; but I know that I may not be able to.

Secondly, I want to tell you what I know of your father. I know you have often been curious, but you have always been such a good girl and have never pushed me when I did not wish to speak of him. Thank you, for that; I am so sorry for not telling you everything.

I was very much in love with your father when I found out I was pregnant, and we had agreed secretly that we would be married. However, he had been betrothed to a woman from his childhood days, and we knew he must officially break this betrothal before we could be wed. Please do not judge me; I promise you that you cannot judge me more harshly than I have myself. All I can say is that I was in love.

However, before I told him I was with child, I realised what he would be giving up to marry me. The woman he was promised to had a dowry, and lands she stood to inherit, and I had nothing. I did not want him to give up everything to be with me - and so I left.

I know it was selfish of me to not think of you more in that moment, and that the simple life we have had to lead has not always been easy. But I did what I felt I must, and I hope you can forgive me.

Your father's name is Rupert Stockwall, and he is currently still the gardener at Marvale. I have not spoken to him since those days, and he does not know of your existence, but he is a good man and I hope he has lived a happy life in the many years since I knew him.

Please forgive me, my darling. I hope you are well, and happy, and that life gives you everything you have ever dreamed of.

I will love you forever.

Your devoted Mama.

My tears had started to fall before I was a third of the way through the letter, and as I reached her heartfelt sentiments at the end of the page I thrust the letter back onto the desk, wrapped my arms around my swollen belly and let the sobs fall. It had been months since I had last cried for my mother, but hearing the words that were as clear as if they were said in her own voice, seeing her plea for forgiveness and her declarations of love for me - it overwhelmed my fragile heart.

Sobs wracked through my body, and when Nicholas found me, curled up on the chair, face puffy and red and tear-stained, he rushed in with a look of horror upon his face.

"Annelise! What is wrong? Are you hurt? Is it the babe?"

I shook my head, reaching around on the desk for the letter and handing it to him. He read silently as tears continued their tracks down my face, before looking back at me.

"So Rupert is definitely your father."

I nodded.

"Oh sweetheart." He held me close as I exhausted myself crying, and when I had calmed down enough to listen he helped me to our bed, loosened the restrictive gown and lay down beside me, holding my body close against his.

"Is there anything I can do, my love?" he asked, pressing his lips to my hair.

I shook my head with a sniff. "My heart just hurts," I admitted.

"I know."

Knowing Rupert was my father, knowing why she had felt she had to leave - it was all information I'd wanted, that would make my life better in the long run. But for now I needed to give in to the pain the reopened wound of grief was causing me, and so I lay in my husband's arms until an exhausted and uneasy sleep took over from tears.

CHAPTER FIFTY-NINE

Nicholas

Six Months Later

Thunder rumbled ominously in the distance, and before long lightening cracked outside the window, sending a shocking flash of white light through the bedroom and causing Annelise to gasp, before turning to smile at me.

Rain lashed against the windows and the panes shook with the force of the wind - but in this room, with the fire burning and our sweet baby boy nestled in his mother's arms, I felt safe and warm.

"He'll sleep through anything," I whispered with a smile, and Annelise rolled her eyes.

"Not when he's in his crib, he doesn't!" she said, and I laughed. She had decided against having little William in the nursery with the nanny, and instead wished to have him in our room, which I had no complaints about. However, it had quickly become apparent that I could sleep through anything - and so it was a constant source of jokes from my wonderful wife.

"To sleep through a storm like this though..." I said, touching his tiny fingers carefully and smiling as they curled up, despite his deep slumber. He was approaching three months old, and I thought I had never seen a happier or healthier little baby.

"He just knows he's safe, and he's loved, so he can sleep peacefully," Annelise said with a soft little smile, as she pressed a kiss to his dark curls.

"He most certainly is," I agreed, leaning back against the pillows with a sigh. "A storm like this reminds me of the day we met!"

"I can't remember any thunder and lightning."

"Well, all right then. The wind and rain were definitely there, though!" I countered.

"Oh, in abundance," she whispered with a laugh.

"And I swept you off your feet, and you fell instantly in love with me," I said, and grinned at her snort in response.

"I think, to begin with, I was rather in awe of you. And then I thought you were plain rude!"

I hummed in agreement, stroking my fingers up and down her arm lazily as I watched William sleeping in her embrace. I was happier than I could have ever imagined, here in this bedroom with my beautiful wife and precious baby. I was happy in every room, in fact; we had worked hard to oversee renovations that I was sure would make my father proud, and thanks to some innovative ideas on Annelise's part, we had worked with the farmers to increase the yields that year.

"I had a letter today," I said, unsure as to what her reaction would be, but knowing it was best to broach it early.

"Oh?"

"From the King."

Her eyes widened a little. "The King of England has written you a letter?"

I laughed. "Well, he probably didn't write it himself," I said. "But I have a letter he has signed, asking me to visit court when it is convenient."

"Oh."

"And I want to take you, and William, and present you to the King."

"Nicholas," she said, her breathing a little uneven, her voice still a whisper to avoid waking our little cherub. "I am a nobody from a backstreet in London. I cannot meet King Henry!"

I pushed myself up off the pillows to meet her lips in a sweet kiss. "You are not a nobody, my dear. You are Lady Gifford of Marvale, and you most certainly can meet the King."

Her eyes fluttered closed, and I fancied it was thanks to my kiss. Then they opened as a small smile played on her lips. "Very well. As long as we don't have to be away from home for too long!"

I grinned; she loved the place as much as I did.

"I promise."

She giggled as another flash of lightening lit up the room.

"I wonder what Father will say at the thought of me meeting royalty!"

"He thinks whatever you do is wonderful," I said. "Never has there been a more devoted father!"

She looked at me and a soft look overtook her features. "I can think of one," she said, and my heart felt like it would overflow with the love I felt for my little family, in this home we had created that was full of happiness, and love, and laughter.

❖ ❖ ❖

Start the next book in the series here: mybook.to/tudorhearts2

AFTERWORD

Thank you so much for reading the first in 'The Hearts of Tudor England' series. I have loved historical fiction for a very long time, but until recently have written contemporary and YA romance. When I decided to take the plunge, it had to be the Tudor era. While I'm not sure I would want to live in such volatile times, I love the drama and the dresses!

I am no historian, just a keen reader and researcher of the period - so please forgive me any anachronisms. I hope you enjoyed Nicholas and Annelise's story as much as I enjoyed writing it; the location of 'Marvale' is based on Cadhay, a beautiful Tudor manor I was lucky enough to get to stay at in August 2020!

You don't have to wait long for the next book in the series: Can't Let My Heart Fall will be released on August 13, and the whole series can be pre-ordered today! Mybook.to/tudorhearts2 .

Finally, a plea: if you enjoyed this book, please consider leaving a review on Amazon or Goodreads. It makes such a difference. If you want to get in touch, feel free to email me at rebeccapaulinyi@gmail.com!

Until the next book - happy reading!

Rebecca

WANT MORE?

Can't get enough of Tudor romance? Get a free short story set in 'The Hearts of Tudor England world' here: https://tinyurl.com/restoremyheart

Read on for a sneak peak at book 2 in 'The Hearts of Tudor England' series: Can't Let My Heart Fall.

BOOK 2: CAN'T LET MY HEART FALL

Queen Katherine's hands danced delicately over the fine shirt she was sewing for her husband, King Henry, as one of the other maids-in-waiting played the lute in the corner of the room. I sat in the window seat, my eyes occasionally drifting out to the courtyard below, where a group of young men were practising their jousting.

The sewing in my own hands lay forgotten in my lap while I watched the group part and bow as King Henry rode out on a magnificent horse, wearing thick furs and an easy smile.

I sat up a little straighter, although of course he could not see me. He was no stranger to the Queen's rooms, and so I had met him - but the frequency of his visits had decreased in the two years since I had come to serve Queen Katherine, and with rumours that he was now courting Anne Bolyen, a former maid of honour like me, those visits diminished even further.

It was too chilly to have the windows open, and so I watched as he shouted something jovial to the young men, before riding off at a pace beyond the castle walls.

My eyes flicked to Katherine, her focus solely on the shirt she was sewing for her husband, and my heart ached a little. Yes, she was the Queen of England. Yes, she had unimaginable wealth and power.

But it seemed she had lost the love of the man she so clearly adored - and the pain of that was clear in her eyes every single day.

As innocent of matters of the heart as I was, I could see the pain love caused her. And that was why, the day before my eighteenth birthday, I had vowed to never fall in love.

I would marry, of course, if God was good enough to provide a husband. I hoped I would raise children and have daughters and sons I could in turn help to marry well.

But I had seen the heartbreak that my mother's death had inflicted on my father, and seen the pain that my mistress went through every day as she saw her husband fall in love with another woman.

And so I vowed, once more, as I picked up my sewing a shoved the needle little too roughly through the thin fabric, that no man would ever win my heart.

It was a pain I would happily live without.

"Alice?" My attention was caught by the sound of my name, and I blushed when I realised Lady Lockwood had been waiting for me to respond.

"Sorry, my lady," I said, ducking my head. I prided myself on excellent service, and it was not like me to let my attention wander.

"Would you read, before mass? Her Grace likes to hear your voice."

I nodded, and made my way to a chair nearer the queen, where a book of poems sat from the previous day. After Mother's death, Father had hired the best governess he could find - and, luckily, had been keen for me to learn reading, writing and even some arithmetic, alongside the traditional wifely arts.

I bowed in a deep curtsy to her, and settled myself in the chair, finding where I had left off before beginning to recite in the clearest voice I could.

I knew some of the other maids of honour - and even the ladies in waiting - could not read as well as I, and my clear voice had caused the Queen to pick me out many times over. She had asked me to write letters for her, too, when there had been none of her closest ladies available, and I felt privileged to have put this great woman's words to paper, to have written to her daughter, the Princess Mary - even if I occasionally caught jealous looks from some of my fellow maids.

I had been reading for almost half an hour when a squire entered, and every head turned in his direction. It used to be common for the Queen to recieve missives from the King, but they were rarer these days. Sometimes ladies would receive a summons from their husband, or their father, or a note from the a prospective husband.

Today, the squire approached, bowed to the queen, and to my surprise passed a note to me before departing, without turning his back on Katherine.

I read the note quickly, before turning to Katherine who was waiting - along with many of the other woman around us - to hear what is said.

"My father has asked that I might attend him, at your earliest convenience, Your Highness."

She smiled at me in a way that made my heart feel more whole than it had done in a long while. It was a mother's smile, and it seemed a travesty that her own daughter were housed so far away and could not bask in its warmth.

"You may go, Alice," she said, a Spanish hint to her voice even after so many years in this country.

"Thank you, your Grace," I said, curtsying before departing, wondering why Father wished to see me. Although we both lived at court, we rarely saw one another, and even more rarely did he seek me out. He was far too busy to be seeing me regularly, and I too busy to be offended.

But if he wanted to see me now, it must be something of import. And the only thing I could think of was the most important event in any young lady's life - the finding of a husband.

As the note had said, he was in his office, where he worked on treaties and letters as part of the Royal Council. I knew his vast knowledge of languages afforded him a privileged place within the King's advisers - after all, that was the reason I had a coveted place in the Queen's household.

"My lord Father," I said, after he had called me in, with a dip of my head to show my respect. He stood and placed his hand on my shoulder for a moment, before sitting back in his chair and gesturing for me to take a seat.

"Alice," he said, a smile on his lips that I had not seen there often. "I hope the Queen was not displeased by my summons."

I shook my head. "She is always very accommodating when our families need us," I said. "And I believe she is pleased with my service."

"That is wonderful to hear. Does she still like to

hear you read?"

I nodded; "In English, Latin and French. And I undertake writing for her too, on occasion."

"Excellent. You are a credit to the family."

I blushed, and belatedly thanked him. Compliments were not handed out lightly by the Duke of Dorset, and I could not remember the last time I had heard one pass his lips - about anyone, let alone me.

"Which brings me to my reason for summoning you here today. I have found you a husband."

Even though I had suspected this might be the reason for his note, I still felt a bubbling in my stomach - a strange mix of nerves and excitement.

The next phase of my life, it seemed, was about to begin.

"Thank you, Father," I answered.

"He is from a good family, and your marriage will forge a powerful allegiance between two of the foremost families of this country."

He spoke with pride, and I felt it in my chest too; I knew how much the family's reputation meant to him. Having one daughter, and no sons, had surely dented his chances of creating a dynasty - but now, if I made an advantageous marriage, perhaps all was not quite lost.

"I am honored," I said, although I ached to know a little more of this man who was to be my husband. "May I know his name?"

"Christopher Danley," he said. "His father is the Earl of Kent."

The son of an Earl... it was a good match. "Is he the eldest son?"

Father smiled, his lips curling wide enough that I could see his teeth.

"Of course."

"If I may make one request," I said, cautiously choosing my words. "I should like to see him before I marry him."

"What difference will that make?" Father asked, with no sympathies for a woman's lack of agency in her life.

"None, I suppose," I said. "Of course I would marry whomever you asked me to. But... I should like to have an idea of who he is before I say my vows."

Father watched me for a moment, and I hoped my words had convinced him. I had always known I would marry whoever was chosen for me - and that the choosing would be even more important because I was an only child, and the child of a

Duke.

I was no rebel; I would not run from a match my father made, nor refuse to say the vows. But before I would belong to this man, I just wanted to lay eyes on him. To know what my future held.

"Strange notions you women have," he said, shaking his head. "Very well. I'm sure I can arrange for him to visit with the Queen and her ladies, and you can set eyes on him then. I do not know if he is yet aware of your name, so say nothing."

I nodded. "Thank you, Father."

"You should be returning to her Grace."

I nodded, and stood, bobbing a curtsy as I left. "Good day, Father."

I took my time wandering back along the corridor, letting his news sink in. I was to be a wife. That was the only detail I really knew; that and the heritage of this man who was to be my husband.

Christopher.

Would he be of an age with me? Or much older? Many women married older men, or widowers - but Father had not mentioned a previous wife, or children for that matter.

I paused at a small, square window to watch the busy goings-on below. I would be a wife, and hopefully a mother. That was always the plan, and now it was being put into motion. I knew I would not allow myself to fall in love with any man - but I did hope he was not too old, and not a cruel man. As long as he was kind, I thought I could get along with anyone.

I just had to wait and see who it was I would be starting the rest of my life with.

Order today: mybook.to/tudorhearts2

BOOKS IN THIS SERIES

The Hearts of Tudor England

Six enchanting stories of love, loss and laughter, set during the Tudor Era.

The Love Of A Lord

When a sudden illness causes grieving hearts to find one another, can love overcome secrets, vows and society's expectations?

Annelise Edwards is compelled to investigate the events leading to her beloved mother's death - but the last thing she expects is to become the guest of the handsome Lord Gifford, at the home where her mother had once worked as a lowly maid.

Lord Nicholas Gifford has no interest in women or falling in love after being jilted by his betrothed. When Annelise appears on his doorstep in a terrible storm and becomes ill, he cannot ignore the sense of duty telling him to take her in until she is recovered enough to be on her way and leave him to the lonely life he has become accustomed to.

But as the stormy days and nights stuck in together force them to share the grief that is weighing on both their hearts, can they deny the attraction that is blooming? Or will the vast difference in their social status stop their romance in its tracks?

The Love of a Lord is book one in The Hearts of Tudor England series, and can be read as a standalone novel.

Can't Let My Heart Fall

When a marriage is arranged for Alice and Christopher, love was never part of the bargain.

Alice Page long ago swore she would never fall in love. After watching her father's heartbreak at the death of her mother, and Queen Katherine's pain at her husband's philandering, it just doesn't seem worth the pain.

Marriage to Christopher Danley, however, makes keeping that solemn vow to herself somewhat difficult. In the daytime she can keep her distance, but at night she realises she has never felt closer to another human before.

Lord Christopher 'Kit' Danley knows he will be an

Earl one day, but he plans to spend every moment of the time before that happens travelling the seas and discovering new lands. When his father delivers an ultimatum, marriage is the only option – but never did he imagine he would find marriage as enjoyable as he does with Lady Alice.

With Alice panicking at realising her heart may be lost to the handsome Kit Danley, and Kit called away on the King's business, can love flourish in this marriage of convenience?

Can't Let My Heart Fall is book two in The Hearts of Tudor England series, and can be read as a standalone novel.

Misrule My Heart

Isabel Radcliffe knows she must marry well. As the daughter of a merchant who has risen at Court, many opportunities are within her grasp - and marrying a Lord is one of them.

When her father hosts nobility over the 12 days of Christmas, she knows she will meet the man he wishes her to marry.

What she does not expect is for him to be so old or unpleasant...

Or to fall in love with a visiting stable lad.

Misrule My Heart is book three in 'The Hearts of Tudor England' series, and can be read as a stand-alone novel.

Saving Grace's Heart

Since witnessing her sister's romantic elopement, Grace Radcliffe has been determined to choose her own husband.

And while finding excuses not to marry every man her father has put in her path has worked so far, she knows time is not on her side - and so she sets her sights on the handsome Duke of Lincoln, planning to ensure they are a good match before letting her father seal the deal.

When Harry, the dashing new Duke of Leicester, is put in her path instead, she knows there must be something wrong with him - for her father has never picked well in the past.

But when he helps her in her hour of greatest need, she begins to question that judgement.

Can Grace find the route to true love? Or will her free-spirited ways lead her into a loveless marriage?

Saving Grace's Heart is Book Three in 'The Hearts

of Tudor England' Series, and can be read as a standalone novel.

Learning To Love Once More

A widowed Earl, a lonely governess, and a whole lot of heartbreak.

James Trant, Earl of Essex, has never known an all-consuming love - but after losing his wife to the perils of childbirth, he resolved not to suffer that pain again.

Fed up of being a burden on her Aunt and Uncle, orphaned Catherine Watt decides being a governess will fill the loneliness in her soul and provide her with a modicum of independence. What she is not expecting is to fall in love with the Earl she is working for.

When James realises he and the children need Catherine in order to flourish, he offers marriage - but in name only. There will be no more children, he is resolute about that.

As Catherine falls deeper and deeper in love with the damaged Earl, can she persuade him that love is worth risking your heart for?

Learning to Love Once More is Book Five in 'The Hearts of Tudor England' series, and can be read as a standalone novel.

An Innocent Heart

On the same day as Henry VIII's second daughter is born, Elizabeth Beaufort makes her way into the world. Inspired by the way the Princess lives her life, she vows to live as a maid - no love, no marriage, no children.

But as the Tudor dynasty sends lives in England reeling, can Bessie Beaufort's heart remain caged?

Edward Ferrers has always known he will marry and carry on his father's merchant business. In fact, such a marriage has been lined up for him for several years - until a chance meeting at the Tudor Court sends his heart racing for Bessie Beaufort.

In a time of courtly love, female purity and religious upset, can Edward persuade Bessie that their love is worth fighting for?

An Innocent Heart is Book Six in 'The Hearts of Tudor England' series, and can be read as a standalone novel.

BOOKS BY THIS AUTHOR

The Worst Christmas Ever?

Can the magic of the Christmas season be rediscovered in a small Devon town?

When Shirley 'Lee' Jones returns home from an awful day at the office, the last thing she expects to find is her husband in bed with another woman. Six weeks until Christmas, and Lee finds the life she had so carefully planned has been utterly decimated.

Hurt, angry and confused, Lee makes a whirlwind decision to drive her problems away and ends up in Totnes, an eccentric town in the heart of Devon. As Christmas approaches, Lee tries to figure out what path her life will follow now, as she looks at it from the perspective of a soon-to-be 31-year-old divorcée.

Can she ever return to her normal life? Or is a new

reality - and a new man - on the horizon?

Finding herself and flirting with the handsome local police officer might just make this the best Christmas ever.

Lawyers And Lattes

A new home, a new man, and a new career are all great - but do they always lead to happily-ever-after?

Shirley 'Lee' Jones has made some spontaneous and sometimes questionable decisions since the breakup of her marriage, but deciding to remain in the quirky town of Totnes has got to be the biggest decision so far. Now Lee has a new business, gorgeous man, and friends keeping life interesting. But when questions of law crop up in her life again, she finds herself yearning for the career and the life plan she gave up when she left everything behind.

And when unexpected news tests her relationship, her resolve, and everything tying her to her life, Lee must decide between the person she is and the person she wants to become.

Sometimes decisions about life, law, and love all reside in grey areas. Will Lee's newfound happiness in Devon be short-lived? Or could her new life give her the chance to have everything she's ever wanted?

Feeling The Fireworks

Can Beth rekindle her passion for life and love in picturesque Dartmouth?

When Beth Davis made a whirlwind decision to move to picturesque Dartmouth to shake up her repetitive life, the last thing she expected to find was a passion in life - or a man who could make her feel fireworks.

A change in home and job seems like exactly what Beth needs to blow away the cobwebs that have been forming around her dead-end job. With little money to her name and no real plan, Beth needs to make things work, fast - without relying on her big sister Lee to bail her out.

When she meets the handsome, mysterious Caspian in a daring late-night swim, she instantly feels fireworks that she had long forgotten. Can Dartmouth - and Caspian - reawaken her passion for life and love?

'Feeling the Fireworks' is Book 3 in the South West Series but can be read as a standalone novel. Fall in love with Devon today!

The Best Christmas Ever

A Devon wedding with the magic of Christmas and a dose of small town charm - and the potential for a lot of family drama.

Lee Davis is about to marry the man of her dreams - and at her favourite time of year. But she's finding it hard to feel the magic of Christmas or the excitement about her wedding as a face from her past reappears and worries about her second time down the aisle surface.

James Knight thought he had everything - the woman he was destined to be with, an adorable daughter and a happy life in the countryside. But with his wife-to-be seeming more and more distant, is he doomed to be jilted at the alter again?

Beth Davis is pretty sure she's lost her heart to handsome, brooding Caspian - but he's moved away to Edinburgh, and their fiery romance seems to have been stopped before it had truly started.

Caspian Blackwell wants to be excited about his promotion and moving to an vibrant new city - but his heart is very much back in Dartmouth.

Can a festive Devon wedding make this the Best Christmas Ever?

Trouble In Tartan

Beth Davis didn't plan on falling in love when she moved to Dartmouth - she just wanted to feel some fireworks. The problem is, she's pretty sure that is exactly what is happening - but the object of her affections is living 600 miles away in Edinburgh. As she tries to start a career as an author, downs a few too many glasses of wine and attempts to make ends meet, keeping a long-distance relationship alive proves more and more challenging.

Caspian Blackwell has never let his heart make big decisions - but he's sorely tempted when the distance between them begins to cause problems in his relationship with Beth. When he decides he wants all or nothing, can he really put this new relationship before his career? Or will he end up exactly where he always feared he would: heartbroken?

A tale of love, longing and a relationship stretched between coastal England and Scotland.

Summer Of Sunshine

A summer holiday can wash up a whole host of family dramas...

Lee Knight wants to relax on a summer holiday

away with her husband, sister and brother-in-law. But her desire for another baby is not making it easy to unwind.

James Knight hates to see his wife upset, and hopes a trip away will make her troubles lessen. But with concerns about his father's health, he's finding it hard to be there for her as much as she really needs.

Beth Blackwell is sick to death of everyone asking her two questions: when is her next book coming out, and when is she going to have a baby. The first is proving more difficult than she expected, and the second - well, she's not sure whether that's the way she wants her life to go.

Caspian Blackwell is enjoying life as a newlywed in Edinburgh - although in his heart, he's missing living in Devon. A spate of redundancies at work has him pondering his future - but he worries his new wife's heart is engaged elsewhere when she becomes increasingly distant.

Can sun, sea and sand send the two couples back into more harmonious waters?

Printed in Great Britain
by Amazon